About the Author

I— as a teacher and parent that Rose Impey first
st— telling her own stories, and they were so well
—ved she soon started writing them down. Rose
—tes fantastic books for all ages – she wrote the
t— selling *Sleepover Club* books for younger readers
— *My Scary Fairy Godmother* and *The Shooting Star*
— two of her wonderful books for older readers.
Rose lives in Leicestershire.

For Rachel and Charlotte

Sincere thanks to:

Diana Wilkes

Dick and Denise Hartley

Michael Impey

LRI Hospital School

and all the wonderful home-educated children I met.

ORCHARD BOOKS
338 Euston Road, London NW1 3BH
Orchard Books Australia
Hachette Children's Books
Level 17/207 Kent Street, Sydney, 2000, NSW, Australia

ISBN 1 84616 215 7
First published in Great Britain in 2006
A paperback original

Text © Rose Impey 2006

The right of Rose Impey to be identified as
the author of this work has been asserted by her in
accordance with the Copyright, Designs and Patents Act, 1988.

A CIP catalogue record for this book is available from the British Library.

1 3 5 7 9 10 8 6 4 2

www.wattspublishing.co.uk

Rose Impey

Hothouse Flower

ORCHARD BOOKS

AB		MO	
MA		MR	
MB		MT	
MC		MW	
MD			
ME			
MG			
MH	·		
MM			
MN			

Chapter One

The day I ran out in front of a bus, and ended up in hospital with a badly broken leg was a lucky day for me. Does that sound completely crazy? Well, it's true. I suppose you might call it a *happy accident.* That's an *oxymoron,* in case you didn't realise, which is where you put two contradictory words together to make more of a point. Yes, I *know* – Grandpa's always telling me – nobody likes a clever devil, but for some reason my brain's full of that sort of stuff.

If it hadn't been for the accident, I might never have discovered the big family secret that everyone had been keeping from me. So, if we're being precise, which I always try to be, I suppose it was *that* that changed my life, more than the accident.

It was a Thursday afternoon in late March, and I was actually riding *on* the bus – the one I later ran out in front of. I was on my way home from my weekly piano lesson – off in my own head as usual, probably imagining myself making some great discovery and becoming fabulously famous!

I almost missed my stop, but I suddenly saw Grandpa's big old black Mercedes parked outside the post office, and him heading towards it. I realised that if I was quick I could get a lift and save myself the long walk home from the village. I was on my feet, hurtling down the aisle of the bus, mumbling, *sorry! sorry! sorry!* as I accidentally bashed people with my music case.

I jumped off the bus, calling across the road, 'Wait for me, Grandpa!'

Even though Marian claims that Grandpa's almost deaf, he must have heard me, because he turned and stood there, with his car keys and a brown paper parcel in his hand, looking straight at me. I remember thinking: I bet I know what's in *that* parcel – more orchid bulbs – Marian won't be pleased.

And then – without another thought – I dashed out.

Grandpa must have already seen the dark blue four-by-four out of the corner of his eye, accelerating to overtake the bus, because he started waving his arms, but he was way too late. He just had to stand and watch the car hit me side-on – with an almighty *Bang!*

Grandpa says he didn't hear the bang, but that's the main thing I remember – like a cannon going off – and the weird feeling that I'd been picked up and then dumped unceremoniously in front of an audience of paper-boys waiting to start their paper rounds. After that, I don't remember *feeling* anything for a while – just a complete sense of nothing.

I don't know how long it lasted but, suddenly, everything seemed to start up again and then complete strangers crowded round me, arguing at the tops of their voices about what needed to happen. They finally agreed that on no account should anyone move me. So I had to go on lying there in the middle of the road, with all the traffic doing a big detour round me, and everyone staring, until the ambulance came.

It was all pretty embarrassing, partly because I'd lost a shoe and my toes were poking through a big hole in my tights. When Grandpa appeared beside me I asked him if he could find it, but it was as if he couldn't understand what I was saying. He looked like he was the one who'd had the accident.

I never did get that shoe back. But then Grandpa lost his parcel of orchid bulbs, too. He must have dropped it in the confusion.

Of course, after that, there were bigger things to worry about than orchids, or lost shoes, or toes poking out of tights: the small matter of bones poking out of legs, for example. I couldn't be sure, because I was too scared to look, but that's what it started to feel like. I couldn't stop shivering, but I didn't actually cry, not even when I saw Grandpa bending over me with tears streaming down his face, which was a surprise, given how things had been between us lately.

I suppose the shock must have taken over next because I passed out. But before I did, the last thing I remember thinking was: perhaps Grandpa does still love me after all.

Chapter Two

Perfection on a Plate

I love the whole idea of PERFECT NUMBERS.
6 is a perfect number, because it is the sum of its factors, which just means the numbers it is divisible by.
1...2...3 are factors of 6 and they also add up to 6!
28 is another perfect number because 1...2...4...7...14 are factors of 28 and also add up to 28.
But, as well as that, both 6 and 28 are the sum of consecutive numbers:
6 = 1+ 2 + 3
28 = 1 + 2 + 3 + 4 + 5 + 6 + 7
How perfect is that? I call that magic!

Ever since I was born, I feel as if I've been surrounded by numbers. There's even a photo of Daniel holding me as a tiny baby in one arm, feeding me a bottle, while doing a complicated equation on a blackboard – as if he's already showing me how to do it.

When I started to talk even my first word was the

number three, although apparently I used to call it *free*. Daniel would point to himself and say, *one*, then to Marian and say, *two*, then to me and say, *three*. Marian says it's a wonder I didn't grow up thinking my name was *Three Wells* – which would have been truly weird.

Daniel's my dad, by the way. He's a mathematician – which is what I'd like to be when I grow up – or maybe an archaeologist. Something famous, anyway.

Daniel's doing research into cryptography, which isn't nearly as exciting as it sounds. I was quite disappointed when I discovered that it has nothing whatsoever to do with spies. It's used for creating codes to keep people's credit cards safe, which sounds pretty boring, but Daniel says the maths isn't.

One of the first things Daniel taught me about was *sets*, which are just groups of things that have something in common, you know, like shapes that are all squares, or even numbers, or people with blue eyes. So, for example, there are three people in the set that makes up the Wells family: Marian, my mum, Daniel, my dad, and me.

Of course, there are times, like at night when I'm in bed, and I can hear Daniel and Marian downstairs on the sofa watching the news with a glass of wine, when

I know that they're the set of adults and I'm not part of that set. But other times it will be Daniel and me – the set of mathematicians, or Grandma and me – the piano players, or Marian and Grandpa – the orchid growers, or Grandpa and Daniel – the football fanatics going to watch Norwich City.

Before Marian married Daniel, she used to be in the Hartley set with Grandpa and Grandma, and her brother Steve. I've never met Uncle Steve and his family. They live in Canada now, and anyway he and Marian haven't spoken in years, so since Grandma died that sort of leaves Grandpa in his own set of *one*. But we usually include him in the Wells set, because he only lives next door.

Even then, *four* still makes a pretty small family and – I'd have to admit it – rather an odd family, too. At least that's what Mary Minchall, who comes to clean for us and Grandpa, often tells me: 'If your Grandma, God rest her soul, could see this place now, she'd turn in her grave: four big brains and not an ounce of common sense between you. It's a wonder you haven't burned the house down already.'

I suppose she has a point: we're always losing things, and breaking things, and forgetting to turn things on or off, especially Daniel – Mr Forgetful.

Marian and I once nicknamed Daniel *The Man who Mislaid his Car* after he drove down into the village to buy a newspaper, started reading it in the shop, and got so involved that he walked the mile and a half home, forgetting he'd taken the car in the first place. The next day Marian thought that it must have been stolen and reported it to the police, who found it within the hour still parked outside the newsagent's! Marian and I couldn't stop laughing. The policeman clearly thought we were all very strange.

Grandpa can be a bit eccentric too, but he doesn't seem to realise it. He just thinks everyone else is odd – especially me.

'Have you noticed all these funny habits Chloe's getting,' he asks Marian.

'Quirks,' Marian corrects him.

'You can call them whatever you like, but they're still not normal.'

'Oh, Dad,' Marian laughs. 'Who wants to be normal, anyway?'

Marian doesn't think normal is anything to aim for. She thinks that normal = ordinary = average = dull. She always tells me to *just be myself.*

'It's fine to be *ab*-normal, as long as you never do anything to hurt anyone else,' she says, but then her eyes fill up and she looks sad, as if someone might have hurt her once upon a time. I certainly can't imagine Marian hurting anyone else.

She doesn't think it matters if I hum when I'm eating. It's a habit, that's all. I don't know why I do it. Or why I only ever wear my socks inside out. Or why I've recently started making chicken noises when I'm close to solving a problem, like I'm about to lay an egg.

OK, I suppose that one is a bit weird.

So you see what I mean, whichever way you look at us – as a group or individuals – you'd probably put us into *the set of very weird people*.

The set of people *outside* my family that I meet regularly is pretty small, too. Apart from Mary Minchall, Mrs Gilbert, my piano teacher, and the appalling Miss Morris, there's really hardly anyone else.

Miss Morris is the person who comes once a year to check up on my education. That's because I don't go to school like other people of my age. I did try it for a while, but it didn't altogether suit me and to be honest I don't think the school knew what to make of *me* either.

In the end Marian and Daniel decided to educate me at home: Daniel does maths; Marian does everything else. She seems to know about all sorts of things and what she doesn't know about we find out together.

When I was little, Marian used to write down all the funny questions I asked like: *How* does an aeroplane full of hundreds of people stay up in the air? or *Why* do trees lose their leaves in winter when they need them to keep warm, and then grow them back in summer when it's warm enough without them? And she put all these questions in what we called the *How?* and *Why?* Box. Then each day we'd take one out and set off on what Marian called a voyage of discovery.

'Come on, Chlo',' she'd say, 'let's have an adventure!' And we'd drive off to a museum, or a Roman ruin, or to the beach to collect fossils, or to a bird sanctuary, and we'd come home bursting to tell Daniel all about it.

Probably my favourite subjects are: reading, history, which I positively worship, geography, and cooking – I *adore* cooking – but if I had to choose, my very best thing is maths. I'm in love with numbers.

Most afternoons I meet up with Daniel to play around with maths for a couple of hours. We don't usually bother with computers. Daniel says that one of the best things about maths is that all you need is a pencil and paper and pure logic. We might talk about things like...*perfect numbers*, for example.

'Just as there are very few perfect people,' Daniel tells me, 'there are very, *very* few *perfect numbers*.'

'How many, exactly?' I ask.

Daniel does what he always does: stops and takes his time before he answers. That's because he likes to be as precise as he can.

'Well, nobody knows *exactly*,' he says. 'The higher you go, the rarer *perfect numbers* become. But, like *natural numbers*, they probably go on to infinity.'

I like things to be a bit more definite than *probably*, but Daniel reminds me that just because a thing hasn't been proved, doesn't mean it isn't true. 'What you must remember about maths, though,' he says, 'is that once something *has* been proved, then it is true – no more question about it – and that never changes.'

That's what I love about maths: you can really rely on numbers, which doesn't mean they're dull and predictable. Numbers are full of surprises. No matter how clever you think you are, because you've cracked some problem or other, they just keep on surprising you, like they're saying: *you think that's impressive, well, wait till you see this.*

Uh-oh, sorry. I have a tendency to burble on a bit, when I get enthusiastic.

Anyway, most days, I get to the kitchen just before four o'clock and make the tea – Earl Grey for Daniel, and a glass of milk for me – and put out a plate of cookies or muffins. Sometimes I might have baked them, if I've been in a messing-around-in-the-kitchen kind of mood. I'm not the best muffin-maker in the world, but even when they don't rise properly, Daniel always says something nice like, 'Mmm, perfection on a plate. I think I might need two of those today,' then he tries unsuccessfully to fit them both in his mouth at the same time!

Daniel says that teatime is a sort of tradition for mathematicians, because they like to share their ideas and often do it over a cup of tea. It's amazing to think that there are people all over the world doing the same thing as us – and some of them at exactly the same time. It feels like being part of a huge family. Probably one of the reasons I like that so much is because my own family is so small. Small, but perfectly formed, Marian says.

As well as teaching me, Marian breeds orchids. She and Grandpa grow them in the nursery next door: Hartley's Heavenly Orchids – *Perfection in a Pot!*

Orchids are still a little unusual in this country, a bit exotic. Some people would say they're the most beautiful flowers in the world and you might think that that would be perfect enough, but Marian says that her aim is to improve on perfection, if she can.

Maths is full of examples of perfection, too, Daniel says. They both tell me how important it is to aim for perfection, even if you fall short of it, because how else are you ever going to achieve it? And I do try, most of the time, because I hate to see either Marian or Daniel upset, or disappointed.

Marian quite often looks upset, but she says that's never anything to do with me. Sometimes she has what I call *droopy days*: she starts off with a funny look in her eyes, like, *hello*, there's no one at home, and then the headaches start and she has to lie in a darkened room for two or three days at a time. She's been having them ever since I was little.

One time I went into her bedroom and found her going through stuff in her bedside drawer, old baby photos and things. She looked quite sad, so

I asked her whether her droopy days started when I was born. But she shook her head. 'Long before that, my darling.'

Then I asked her what I'd been like as a baby, and she said, 'Absolutely perfect,' but that seemed to make her even more droopy. I couldn't understand it but I decided it must be a grown-ups' thing.

I bet you're wondering: with not going to school and with only Marian and Daniel around, don't I ever get lonely? People often ask me that. But I find there's always plenty to do – if you've got a good imagination and an active brain. I don't seem to have time to get lonely. In fact, I often think how lucky I am that I'm not locked up in a classroom day after day. I can do exactly what I want to do, whenever I want to do it. I can even go a bit crazy, if I feel like it – especially when there's no one to see me, like when I'm on The Log!

The Log is my special place. It's at the very bottom of my garden and it's where I go when I need to do a bit of what I call *mind-wiping*, like when my head's bursting with a maths problem I can't solve, or when all I feel like doing is dreaming, or just *being ME* – when I don't particularly want to be good, or right or *perfect.*

When I tell Grandpa what Marian and Daniel say about perfection, he rolls his eyes and groans.

'For goodness' sake,' he growls, 'children aren't like hothouse flowers. They don't need to be perfect – good enough will do,' which is a bit of a relief, to be honest.

Chapter Three

That first night in hospital, after my accident, I lost any sense of time; it seemed to go on for days. I couldn't separate out what was really happening from the very strange dreams I was having.

I'd arrived in the ambulance – no flashing lights and siren, disappointingly – with my leg in a vacuum splint, and already attached to a drip, with an oxygen mask over my face, which I hated. I was X-rayed and examined by two or three different doctors, and that all happened quite quickly. They asked me some questions to make sure I wasn't concussed, but once they gave me the painkillers everything went into slow motion and people's faces and voices kept moving out of focus.

I knew where I was, most of the time, but I kept finding myself falling into a deep sleep, a bit like disappearing down a huge hole. One time, when I came back to the surface, I seemed to be in a dimly lit tunnel sailing very slowly one way – with the rest of the world moving just as slowly in the opposite direction. I knew that my mum and dad and grandpa were somewhere nearby, because I could hear them talking, but they always sounded just out of reach.

The nurses woke me up and gave me more painkillers, so that the doctor could set up the traction to immobilise my broken leg. I'm sure I would have found it all absolutely fascinating if it had been happening to someone else, but I just wanted them to go away and leave me alone and let me go back to sleep.

The doctor put my leg in a Thomas splint, which hurt a lot, even with the painkillers, then he and the nurse attached the splint to a set of ropes and pulleys over my bed to keep it from moving. I tried to make a joke, and told the doctor it looked like something they used in the Dark Ages, but he didn't even smile. The nurse smiled though and said, 'Don't worry, Chloe, we're saving the thumb screws for later.'

I was glad she had a sense of humour at least. Anyway, I thought, things can't be too bad if she's making jokes about it, and Daniel picking me up on my language was another good sign.

When I said an instrument of torture described it pretty precisely, Daniel said, 'Come on, Chloe, either something's precise or it isn't. It can't be *pretty precise*, can it?' But he was smiling and stroking my hair when he said it, so I knew he didn't care. After all, I had broken my femur in five different places. *Shattered* was the word the doctor used, which made it sound more like glass than bone.

Marian sort of gasped and for a minute we all thought she was going to faint. 'I can't bear it,' she sort of whispered.

'Don't worry, Mrs Wells,' the doctor told her. 'She's a very lucky young lady. Despite making an excellent job of shattering her femur, she doesn't seem to have caused any other real damage. Fortunately it didn't actually break the skin. There's some serious bruises that she'll know all about tomorrow, though.'

I felt like saying, 'I didn't manage this on my own, you know, there was a huge great car involved too,' but I couldn't find the energy to bother. I just drifted off again, while he was still talking.

In a half-dream, I was floating somewhere, a little

way away, sort of there but not there. It was quite a nice feeling actually. I could hear little snatches of conversation; quite reassuring bits like: *I can promise you: nobody's going to die,* and: *No serious internal damage.* And then some bits that weren't quite so cheery: *We can't rule out an operation further down the line. She'll be on traction for four to six weeks.* And: *She's in the best place, I can assure you.*

After that I must have floated off altogether because I had a very weird kind of dream where I'm at home, in the garden, back on The Log. Maybe it isn't my Log, because it suddenly seems to stand up on end and turn into a giant with eyes like headlamps. And it picks me up, and starts throwing me up in the air and catching me, like I'm a ball, over and over again as if it's trying to break its own record. There are people lined up watching and cheering and I'm thinking, I wish it would hurry up and finish because it must be four o'clock by now, time to make tea for Daniel. He'll be waiting in the kitchen, wondering where I am, and Marian will get worried and then and then...

And then I was back in the hospital, because someone – Marian I think – was clutching my hand so tightly it was hurting. I tried to pull my hand away, but I didn't have the strength and I think I must have drifted off again.

This time I'm in my bedroom and I'm having a different dream where I'm wrestling with a very difficult maths problem. It's really frustrating because every time I think I have the answer, before I can write it down, it disappears. So I have to go back and rework it all and then the same thing happens, as if there's a hole in my brain and things keep escaping. It's absolutely maddening anyway and I want to scream but when I do no sound comes out – nothing at all.

Then I was back in the hospital, on the paediatric ward now, and I was half awake, hearing voices again, quiet but cross voices, and I knew it must be Marian and Grandpa (they're always the ones arguing), and then Daniel's voice, calming them down as usual.

I should never have let her go on that bus – not on her own.

Why do you always have to blame yourself, Marian? It was just as much my fault – and that wretched piano's!

No, it was *my fault. I knew it was a mistake.*

It's no one's fault, Marian. Accidents happen. Things go wrong.

Someone was sobbing and I knew that had to be Marian. Poor Marian, I wanted to squeeze her hand and tell her, I'm OK, you don't have to worry, but she seemed too far away. And, anyway, it was suddenly too much effort. I heard Daniel say he was going to get them all a cup of coffee, and I drifted off again.

Now I'm in the jungle and it's wonderful. There are orchids all round me, smelling like chocolate, and honey, and *coffee*, at least I think they're orchids, but in my experience no orchids, not even Grandpa's, smell anything like this. Most of Marian's don't smell at all.

Now Grandma is with me. She takes my hand and asks me, 'What's the first thing you do, Chloe, when you see a beautiful flower?' But this seems such a difficult question and I don't know the answer. 'You put your nose into it, of course,' she tells me. 'How can Marian talk about perfection, when she's missing the most important thing? No point raising peoples' expectations, only to disappoint them. Make sure you tell her that, won't you, Chloe?'

I could feel tears then for the first time, thinking

how much I missed my grandma. I really wished she were in the hospital with us. She'd have stopped Marian and Grandpa from arguing. I could still hear them, somewhere nearby.

I've never understood why it always had to be such a secret.

Oh, don't start on that, Dad, not now, for goodness sake.

But it was all so long ago…

Dad, please…

It wasn't her fault. So why's she had to pay for it?

Marian was crying again. I wished Daniel would come and then she would stop.

I wondered who they could be talking about, but the next moment I couldn't even remember what they'd said, because that hole in my brain seemed to be getting bigger and more things were disappearing. The harder I tried to hold onto them the faster they were gone. In the end my brain was completely empty and I must have fallen properly asleep.

Hours later, when the nurse woke me to take my pulse and temperature, and check the pressure on the splint, I thought that must be another dream, but then I remembered where I was and why I was there. I got really scared then because I could hardly move my head; it felt as if it weighed a ton. Every inch of my body seemed to be hurting.

Everyone else had gone, except Marian who was asleep on a little camp bed beside me. It was really dark on the ward, and yet the one or two lights there seemed to be shining right in my eyes. I could hear babies crying all round me, which made my head ache even more. I couldn't understand where they'd all come from.

When she was finished checking me, the nurse bent over and whispered, 'How are you feeling? Do you need anything, Chloe? Can I get you a drink?'

But I was far too tired to speak. I shook my head, which only made it throb even more, so I closed my eyes and let myself disappear again down that deep, deep hole.

Chapter Four
The Power of Three

Nature really seems to love the number three!
Orchids, for example, have three petals, three
sepals, three stamens, and three carpels.
And, in order to survive, orchids also form
part of a triangle – flower – insect – fungus.
The orchid needs the insect – usually a bee,
butterfly or moth – to pollinate it, and
fungus to provide the nutrients it needs. But
the insect and fungus need the orchid to
survive too.
It's what you call a SYMBIOTIC RELATIONSHIP.

One good thing about being home-schooled is – you don't have far to go, and another is – you don't have to be there for nine o'clock. You just start when you feel like it, which is good for me because I'm not exactly what you'd call a morning person.

Once I'm awake, I grab myself some breakfast and

go and find Marian in her lab, to talk about what I'm going to do that day.

I'd have to admit that *lab* makes it sound a bit grand, when it's really just an extension that Grandpa and Daniel built on the side of the garage. It has long workbenches, with a microscope and other bits of equipment and an autoclave, for sterilising everything – bacteria are one of the main enemies for orchid breeders – and shelves full of tiny flasks of orchid cultures and thousands of seedling orchids at different stages of growth. Baby orchids need exactly the right temperature and humidity and seem to need looking after like real babies.

Sometimes, if I can see Marian through the glass panel in the door, already bent over her microscope, I might go and pootle around for a bit before I disturb her, or go and pester Grandpa in the hothouses. Sometimes it feels like *we're* a bit of a *symbiotic triangle*, because whichever one of them I'm with, you can bet they'll be complaining to me about the other one.

This is a fairly typical kind of conversation I might have with Marian:

'So, what have you been up to?' she asks, giving me a morning hug.

'Helping with the weeding,' I tell her. 'Grandpa says it's like painting the Forth Bridge. By the time he gets to the end he has to start back at the beginning.'

'If Grandpa doesn't like weeding he should never have chosen *Stanhopeas* to specialise in,' she says, grinning and peering over her glasses.

Most orchids, like Marian's, grow in bark, so they don't need weeding, but Grandpa says his are such *big babies* they need extra nutrient. That's why he grows them in sphagnum moss – which weeds just love.

I remind her what Grandpa always says, that you don't choose your orchids – they choose you.

Marian sighs and rolls her eyes. 'Why would anyone *choose Stanhopeas*? They're so big, they take up so much room, and, let's face it, they're never going to win a beauty contest.'

I don't tell Marian what Grandpa says about *her* orchids: that *Phalaenopsis* are the Barbie dolls of the orchid world.

'They're just house plants for housewives,' he says, looking down his nose. 'They're not *orchid-growers'* orchids.'

Marian and I think Grandpa's a bit of an orchid snob. He holds the National Collection of *Stanhopeas* in this country, which means he has one of almost every species that's ever been discovered anywhere in the world. He only needs four or five more to complete it. But Marian thinks that Grandpa's obsessed with his collection, especially since Grandma died.

'What your grandfather seems to forget is that this is a business we're running – not a hobby. Personally, I can't see anything wrong with just trying to produce beautiful plants at a price people can afford, and plants that stand half a chance of surviving once they're taken home.'

I can't help smiling, because I've heard this speech before.

Marian smiles back. 'Anyway, your grandfather needs to be careful, otherwise one of these days he'll find himself in prison on bread and water, and he'll only have himself to blame.'

I probably *shouldn't* have told Grandpa that! If you get him started on what he calls *the orchid police* (they're the officials from CITES – the organisation that controls the movement of orchids around the world), he looks like he could burst a blood vessel.

'The problem, Chloe,' he explains, 'is that every day whole species of orchids die out in countries like

Peru and Chile, simply because their habitats are being wiped out to make way for logging and mining. The greed of big business is doing far more damage than all the orchid collectors in the world put together. And do you know the worst part?'

I nod, because he's told me lots of times, but he still tells me again.

'Because of their silly regulations, they won't let a single plant be removed before the logging starts. They're just ploughed up – thousands and thousands of rare orchids! It's madness! Utter lunacy. If they'd just allow a few to be exported – to dedicated growers like me – we could breed from them, then there'd be no conservation problem. But instead those *idiot officials* stand aside and allow them to be destroyed.'

I can see Grandpa's point of view, and I know that Marian can too. Of course she won't admit it, partly in case it encourages him to break the law, but partly because she and Grandpa seem to like to disagree on principle – and guess who usually gets stuck in the middle.

Grandpa tells me all sorts of things that I'm not supposed to tell Marian, or at least, he used to. But that all changed after we had our big argument.

It was on a warm, sunny day last year, a few months after Grandma died. I'd wandered next door in a full-of-the-joys-of-June kind of mood thinking that Grandpa might like some company. I probably should have known better – he'd been far grumpier since Grandma died.

I balanced my bowl of Weetabix in one hand, while I slipped into a pair of wellingtons, before I went into the hothouse. Grandpa gets irritated if I wander round in my bare feet, particularly when he's been watering.

The heavy rich smell of orchids came out to meet me and I just breathed it in. That first noseful always seems so wonderful and *exotic*. But when you've been in there a while, it's not such a great smell, especially mixed with Grandpa's cigars. He's supposed to have given up smoking – and he had until Grandma died, then he started again. (That's something else I'm not supposed to tell Marian.)

I've never been in a jungle myself, but that's what I imagine it must be like: hot and steamy, with plants hanging down, dripping on your head, hundreds more at eye level, and even more packed onto the benches, spilling almost down to the floor. It's just a sea of green, with splashes of colour, some vibrant, but others soft and pale. Grandpa's other favourite orchids are called *Lycastes* and when they're in flower they look a bit like pale pink babies in bonnets. Or to be more precise little aliens in bonnets, which looks almost as weird as it sounds.

This particular day Grandpa was bent over the benches potting up tiny little seedlings using a pair of tweezers. He didn't look up when I came in.

'Uh-oh, keep your heads down,' he muttered, '*Trouble* has just entered the building.' Grandpa often talks to his orchids.

'Morning, Grandpa,' I said.

'*Listen* to her! She calls this *morning*. Nearer lunchtime I'd say. What a life! It must be lovely to laze in bed half the day and then please yourself the rest.' I just smiled and carried on eating my Weetabix. 'And she's not even dressed yet.' He shook his head as if he completely despaired of me.

Grandpa spent years as a dentist in the army and he's very keen on discipline. He says the whole world has gone soft and the fact that I occasionally spend a whole day in my pyjamas and bare feet only proves it.

'Haven't you got any lessons to be doing?'

'Yes, loads,' I said. 'But I thought I'd say hello, before I got started.'

Grandpa humphed. He thinks I spend far too much time *pootling* around and I'd be better if I had more routine to my days.

He'd been labelling some new plants earlier and I couldn't help noticing he'd spelled one or two of the labels wrong. Grandpa's eyesight isn't as good as it was, but he refuses to wear his glasses because he says the humidity steams them up. Marian says he just doesn't want to admit he's getting old.

'You've missed a letter out here, Grandpa,' I told him.

He pretended he hadn't heard and I should have just left it but, as you've probably guessed, I didn't.

'*Stanhopea tigrina*,' I said, 'you've missed the "r" out.' He still didn't answer so I picked up a marker pen.

Grandpa stopped weeding, checked the labels then threw them irritably across the bench. He took the pen off me. 'I'll do it,' he snapped. 'I want to be able to read it.'

Grandpa has beautiful writing – copperplate it's called – and he tried to teach me once because he said my writing looked as if a spider had crawled in a pot of ink and then died on the page. He sometimes criticises my spelling too – which isn't always perfect. I know it's just his way and I'm used to it, but he never usually shouts at me, so I wasn't expecting this: 'It's time you learned, young lady, that nobody likes a clever devil, least of all me!'

I wasn't meaning to be a clever devil, and that really hurt. I hardly ever lose my temper – but that day I shouted back at him, 'I'm not a clever devil, but I *was* right about the piano key. I know where Grandma kept it.'

Grandma had been teaching me to play the piano and I used to go round every day to practise. After she died, Marian said I should give Grandpa a bit of space. A few months later, when things were getting back to normal, I asked if I could start to play again, but when Marian asked Grandpa he said he'd locked the piano and now he couldn't find the key.

Well, I knew where there was a spare one, but Grandpa told Marian I was wrong – there had never been a spare. And that was the end of it.

'It was in her jewellery box,' I shouted at him.

'I know because she showed me.' And I started crying, because at that moment I really missed her.

I could tell that Grandpa did too, because he suddenly looked very old and sad. 'Contrary to popular opinion,' he said, 'you don't know everything, Chloe! In fact, it's a tragedy, some of the things you don't know.' And he turned away and went back to his planting.

I had no idea what he meant by that, because obviously there were lots of things I didn't know – I was only eleven for goodness' sake. But looking back, that was a clue, if I'd only realised it.

Later, when I told Marian that Grandpa had snapped at me, she said, 'Join the club. He's just got a sharp tongue sometimes, especially since Grandma died. I'm sure it was nothing to do with you, sweetheart.'

I supposed that Marian was probably right, but after that things weren't quite the same between us. I didn't feel like I could go round there so often. It's a shame, because when I was younger Grandpa used to call me *his best little helper*. After that it started to feel like I hadn't only lost my grandma, I'd sort of lost my grandpa too.

Anyway, by then Grandpa was spending more and

more time in his office, on his computer, talking by e-mail to other orchid growers in Canada or the Czech Republic or Vietnam. It seems that orchid growers are like one big family, too.

'There's something a bit crazy about orchid people,' Grandpa once told me. 'It's like we've all been bitten by the same bug and caught orchid fever.'

It can be a dangerous thing to catch. Apparently a hundred years ago, when orchids were *really* fashionable, it was often fatal. Orchid hunters shot or stabbed one another to be the first to find new species. Sometimes hunters were bitten by snakes, or trampled by cattle, or charged by rhinoceroses, or fell out of trees while they were searching for rare plants, or had plants fall on *them*. One orchid from Borneo is so big and heavy that collectors have been knocked out by it – even squashed to death!

Fortunately, it's not like that nowadays. For most people – like Grandpa and Marian – being an orchid lover isn't exactly dangerous, it just makes you sort of...*odd*.

Marian had been especially odd since Grandma died. Her droopy days turned into weeks – and she was worse than droopy. I couldn't really understand why she took it so badly, because Grandma had been ill for a long while and we all knew deep down that she was going to die. Of course all of us were sad, but Marian just went to pieces, as if she hadn't seen it coming.

When I was little, I once asked Grandpa whether it was because of orchid fever that Marian had her droopy days, and couldn't the doctor give her some medicine for it, but he said it was nothing to do with orchids. His eyes were full of tears, though, so I knew better than to ask any more questions.

Anyway, a few weeks after our big argument, Grandpa sort of admitted I was right because a piano key finally turned up. The piano was moved into our house and Marian and Daniel decided to let me have piano lessons with Mrs Gilbert who lives a few miles away in Lower Wittering – which is a wonderful name, don't you think?

Then, when Marian realised I'd have to walk a mile and a half to the village and catch a bus to Mrs Gilbert's – all on my own, it almost didn't happen. There was this big family conference to discuss all the possible dangers. You'd have thought I was embarking on an expedition up the Amazon, at least. Marian insisted on going with me the first few times, but then Daniel intervened.

Luckily Daniel isn't such a worrier as Marian and he managed to persuade her that I was perfectly safe to be let out on my own – which is how I came to be on the bus that day – and then run out in front of it.

I remember lying in bed a few nights hearing them arguing about it.

'If Chloe went to school she'd have much farther to travel than that,' Daniel pointed out.

'But she doesn't have to, thank goodness, which is one of the advantages of keeping her at home, surely.'

'Lots of girls her age do, though, Marian, and manage just fine.'

'But what if anything happens to her? I'd never forgive myself!'

Marian often says things like that, whereas Daniel often says things like: 'You know how sensible Chloe is.'

And most of the time I am.

'Come on, Marian,' Daniel said finally, quietly but

firmly. 'Chloe will be twelve next birthday, we ought to be letting her out more. And she can't come to much harm over that short distance.'

Oh dear, famous last words. I bet poor old Daniel had to eat those.

Chapter Five

Hospitals are really noisy places. I don't know how people ever get better in them. The nurses wake you incredibly early. I'm never up at seven o'clock normally! I was still half asleep when my bed started to move. I thought this must be another dream and I'm riding along a railway track. But it wasn't a dream. They were moving my bed into a side ward, which was like a room on my own.

I could tell there was something funny going on because Marian and the nurses weren't even looking at each other and there was an atmosphere you could have cut up and weighed.

Once the nurses had gone, Marian said, 'Well, if we're going to have to stay in this place we can at least get some privacy. You'd never have got better out there, among all that sickness and noise – and who knows what deadly germs. Anyway, I can't understand their problem; no one was using it.'

Apparently Marian had been arguing with the nurses for over an hour about the room but she'd got her way in the end and I have to admit, it *was* much nicer and quieter in there.

'How are you feeling, my darling?' she asked me.

I was feeling like I'd been thrown down the road by a speeding four-by-four, which I had, and as if I'd broken every bone in my body, which fortunately I hadn't. The doctor had been right about the bruising, every little bit of me felt sore, but I didn't want Marian any more worried about me than she was already.

'I've felt better,' I said and even managed a smile.

'You've looked better,' she said stroking my face.

So had she, she looked *terrible*, but I thought I'd better not tell her that.

She told me that Daniel was coming in later to bring her a bag of things and was there anything in particular I wanted? I couldn't even think about it, but when I closed my eyes I suddenly said, 'My pink hat!' I needed something snuggly to cheer me up.

Marian squeezed my hand. She looked as if she was going to cry again, and I didn't want her to start me off. 'Things could be worse,' I said. 'At least my hair's not on fire,' which was one of Grandma's sayings.

'Oh, Chloe, you gave us all the fright of our lives. I'm not sure that Grandpa will ever get over it. He said it was like a nightmare – just having to watch it all happen and not being able to do anything to stop it.'

Poor old Grandpa, I suppose it must have been horrible for him too.

The nurse came back in then to check my temperature and pulse and stuff. She gave me some more painkillers. After that I must have drifted off again – back down the hole.

When I woke up I felt a lot better. There was a new nurse who'd just come on duty, called Jo, who was tidying my bed. She told me that Marian had gone for a shower. The next minute the room was full of people: a consultant called Mr Clarke, and his three students. They were talking about me as if I wasn't even there and calling me *this little girl*!

'I'm nearly twelve,' I said, then I held out my hand, so he'd know I wasn't being rude.

Mr Clarke looked surprised, but then he shook my hand and smiled back.

'What's going to happen to me?' I asked.

'Well, you're going to have to stay on traction for a while, I'm afraid.'

'How long is a while?' I asked. 'Could you be more precise?'

I noticed Jo smiling, and all the students grinning behind their notebooks.

'It's difficult to *be* precise,' he replied, grinning too. 'Your femur's fragmented...'

'The other doctor said it was *shattered*,' I interrupted.

Mr Clarke raised his eyes. 'Well, it means pretty much the same. So it rather depends on how quickly you heal.'

'I don't know about that,' I told him, 'I've never broken anything before.'

'Then it'll be a learning experience for both of us,' he smiled. 'I could make an educated guess and say...four to six weeks – just as long as you don't hold me to it and then sue me.'

'OK,' I said. 'It's a deal.' I always like people with a sense of humour.

'But don't worry, Chloe,' he said, 'we'll find plenty to occupy you; we won't let you get bored.'

'Oh, I never get bored,' I said. 'Marian and Daniel make sure of that.'

'Are they your brother and sister?' he asked.

'No,' I said laughing. 'My mum and dad.'

Mr Clarke gave me one of those funny looks that I've seen adults give me before, as if they're thinking: what a very strange person! which in some ways I suppose I am.

Just then Marian came back from the shower and introduced herself. Her hair was still wet and I think she was a bit embarrassed. In no time she was raising her voice and asking Mr Clarke exactly why I couldn't be looked after at home.

'I'm afraid that *really* wouldn't be advisable,' he said firmly.

'But Chloe's not like other children,' Marian said, almost in tears. 'She's never been away from us. She won't survive in here. She *needs* to be at home.'

I wished Marian wouldn't say things like that. She made me sound even weirder than I am. I could see Mr Clarke beginning to look irritated.

'I'm sure *Chloe* will survive perfectly well,' he said. 'You really needn't worry about her, Mrs Wells. While she's here she'll be well looked after.'

He left Jo to explain to us that she was my named nurse, which meant that she'd be the one to make sure my treatment went well and if we had *any* worries she was the person to sort them out.

I felt a bit sorry for Jo because Marian's face looked as if her list of worries might be endless. But, actually, if anyone looked as if they might be able to handle Marian, Jo did.

I'm not always good at working people out, because, obviously, I haven't had a lot of practice – but Jo looked to me like an interesting mixture: very kind and smiley, and yet she had a way of holding her head on one side when she looked at you that made you think you'd better not try to pull the wool over *her* eyes.

With her dark skin and big smile, standing next to Marian, who was looking smaller and paler and more wobbly than usual, Jo seemed like the smiliest, solidest person in the world.

The rest of the day my room felt like Paddington station – Marian and Daniel took me there once on a trip to London and it was the busiest place I've ever seen. One after another, people kept popping in and out of my room, introducing themselves, asking questions, doing assessments.

There was a dietician and a physiotherapist, and then a lady who came and took my blood, although she called it *bloods,* which I didn't understand. And a pressure area care nurse to make sure I didn't get pressure sores, because I'd be staying in bed for a month. I couldn't imagine what that was going to be like – lying in bed for a whole month – or maybe even longer!

Marian had slipped down to the cafeteria to get a sandwich when the next visitor came. Gemma was a really pretty girl with a big smile, who kept laughing at her own jokes.

'I'm the Play Specialist on the ward, Chloe,' she said, 'just in case you want someone to play with. Hee, hee, hee. I'll be popping in and out, but if ever you want me just send a message. I've got lots of activities I can bring along here for you. Do you like painting? I'm a bit of a collage-nut, myself. Not really, just joking. Hee, hee, hee.'

She must have seen the look on my face, because art is *not* my favourite thing – I don't really get it – but she wasn't a bit put off. 'Oh, don't worry, I've got lots more fab ideas where they came from. I'll make sure you never get bored.'

Everyone did seem obsessed with me getting bored. It was a good job Marian wasn't there. She's got quite strong ideas on that subject herself.

Gemma asked me who was my named nurse and when I said, Jo, she leaned forward and whispered something that suddenly broke my dream: 'I'll let you into a little secret, Chloe. All the nurses here are lovely, but Jo's the very best.'

There had been something in my dream about secrets. I struggled to get hold of it again. Marian, and I think Grandpa, had been there and I'd been floating over their heads, like a big bird, eavesdropping, but I couldn't remember what it was about. I thought, I must ask Marian when she comes back, but by then it had gone completely out of my head, because I had another visitor: Mrs Bryce-Jones. She was very nice too. She told me that she worked in the hospital school. I was surprised, because I never knew that there *was* such a thing.

She told me that lots of children were taken there each day from the wards, and lots of other children who'd already gone home came in for the day in taxis, if they still weren't well enough to go to normal school. Obviously I wouldn't be able to go along there, because I was on traction. Instead a teacher would come every day and give me work to do, starting tomorrow if I felt up to it. She said that they would devise my own personal scheme of work, unless my school sent in work for me.

I'd just started to tell her that I didn't actually go to school, when Marian came back. She'd had a lot of trouble trying to buy anything in the café that wasn't on white bread or full of E-numbers, so she wasn't in the best mood already.

Mrs Bryce-Jones started to explain again why she'd come but Marian just cut her off. 'No! Thank you!' she said, as if the teacher was trying to sell her something. 'Chloe doesn't need any schemes of work.'

Mrs Bryce-Jones took a deep breath, you could see she was trying to keep her temper. 'We are required by law, Mrs Wells, to provide every child with the opportunities for learning throughout their stay in the hospital...'

Marian looked too tired to argue, but she said, 'I know you have a job to do, and I understand that, but my husband and I have elected to educate our daughter ourselves, which is absolutely our right within the law and we have never, nor do we now, require any assistance. Thank you.'

I felt quite sorry for the teacher who left looking a bit red in the face. After she'd gone Marian seemed to deflate like a balloon. She hates arguing with anyone. I couldn't understand why she'd got so cross. She was starting to look a bit worrying to be honest.

'I hate hospitals,' she said, suddenly.

'It's not that bad,' I said, trying to cheer her up. 'At least we've got a room of our own.'

But it was as if she wasn't listening to me.

'I've got to get you out of here,' she kept on.

'I don't think Mr Clarke will be very happy about that,' I told her.

'I should never have let you out of my sight,' she groaned. 'This is all my fault.'

I seemed to remember hearing Marian say that the night before, which reminded me about my dream – and the secret I thought I'd heard Grandpa mention. But Marian's eyes were full of tears and she was looking so anxious again that I was scared of making things worse.

I couldn't understand why she seemed so worried when everyone was telling us that I was going to be fine. I thought it must be because she was tired and suddenly I realised that I was too.

We both must have dozed off after that, because Jo woke us up when she came in with a message from

Daniel to say that he was sorry he'd been held up – Grandpa wasn't too good. He felt sure it was nothing serious and he'd come in as soon as he could.

Jo did what she called *obs*, which is short for observations, I suppose: checked my pulse, my respiration rate and temperature, then she checked the tension on the traction again.

'OK, Chloe, that's you sorted for now, unless I can get you anything?'

I shook my head. 'No, thanks.'

'I'm going off duty shortly, but another nurse will look in on you soon.'

'I'll see you tomorrow,' I said and smiled.

Jo smiled back. 'God willing,' she said.

I noticed the look on Marian's face and hoped that Jo hadn't. It was just a sort of rolling of the eyes, but I knew what it meant. Marian and Daniel are atheists, they don't believe in God, they think it's all superstition. They only believe in things that can be proved.

As Jo was leaving, a girl about my age, with the most incredible hairstyle, was passing the door in a wheelchair. Jo just turned back towards me and said, 'Chloe, this is Delia. Anything you want to know about hospital routines, ask Delia. She's an old hand.'

Delia sat in her wheelchair in the doorway and grinned at me. She gave me a little wave. I sort of lifted my hand but I didn't quite know what to do with it, so let it drop again. I quickly looked across at Marian, who got up and walked to the door. She smiled at Delia but closed the door behind Jo without saying anything.

Marian didn't need to say anything to me either. We both know I'm not very good with other kids. I don't mind babies; babies don't make you feel as if you're weird. I don't mind watching other kids from a distance, but close up they make me nervous.

I was even more relieved that Marian had won the argument to get me a room on my own. Stuck in bed, with my leg in traction, I felt a bit like a sitting target. At least now we had a door we could close.

Chapter Six

Perfectly Natural?

In the beginning, for the purpose of counting, people only used whole numbers.

These were called NATURAL NUMBERS: 1, 2, 3, 4...

These numbers allowed a man to count how many sheep he owned. They also allowed him to multiply. If he had 3 sheep and each had 2 lambs, the man could calculate that he had 6 lambs altogether.

They were enough for simple subtraction too.

If he had 8 sheep and 2 died, the man was left with 6 sheep, for example.

But sharing sheep proved a bit more tricky.

8 sheep ÷ 2 men wasn't a problem, but 2 sheep ÷ 8 men suddenly required the invention of fractions. Fractions weren't considered to be natural numbers, which seems a bit hard on fractions, I think.

Orchids are one of the largest plant families in the world. They're found in every continent, from the equator to the poles. Most people think that orchids are really exotic and – because many come from hot, steamy places – that they're tricky plants to grow here. But Grandpa says it's partly a question of acclimatisation. Given a bit of time, and the right conditions, most orchids adapt perfectly well, he says, even when they're moved half way across the world, whereas others moved only a matter of metres won't thrive if one important element – like the symbiotic fungus, for example – is missing.

I'm not sure what important element was missing in my case, when I came to go to school, but even though I went for nearly two years, I never managed to acclimatise.

I can still remember lots of things about it: falling asleep in an afternoon in the book corner and the teacher's perfume and the taste of warm milk, but the thing I remember most of all was the noise. I remember standing in the playground with my hands over my ears wondering why everyone was yelling at each other and wishing they would stop.

The teacher gave me a first reading book about two characters called Biff and Chip, but later that day, when she heard me reading out all the credits at the end of a TV programme, she gave a big sigh and took it off me again. She never seemed to know what to do with me after that, although she was very nice. It wasn't the teachers I was nervous of.

Marian says that every morning I would go straight into the classroom and sit at a table, all on my own, doing puzzles. I can't really remember that, but I can remember looking back and seeing her watching me through the window with this really sad face – and the fact that she was always the first mum there, at the end of the day, waiting to collect me. One day, after two years, when I was still standing at the gate on my own every morning saying, 'Do I really have to go?' Marian said, 'No, you don't,' and we turned right round and came home.

We were both happier after that. Whereas Daniel easily goes off to conferences and meetings all over the world, Marian and I feel happier back at home. You could say that's our natural habitat, where we both thrive.

Each morning Marian would ask, 'So, what kind of a day is it today?' And depending on what mood I was in, I would choose.

I've always been quite a 'mood' kind of person, which I think is altogether different from being a *moody* kind of person. Since I was little I've always liked to dress for the mood I wake up in. For example, I might sometimes be in a dreamy, floaty, hippy sort of mood, then I'd wear a long skirt and sandals and a floppy hat. I have a thing about hats, by the way. You could say I'm a bit of a hat-aholic.

Very occasionally I wake up in a sporty, energetic, Tiggerish kind of mood and put on a tracksuit and trainers and a baseball cap and race about the garden, maybe climbing trees, or building something preposterous.

Or some days I might wake feeling sharp and determined to be focused all day on my work. Then I'll wear a shirt and skirt and a pair of glasses I've got that have no glass in them but make me feel especially clever and studious.

I *love* dressing up; it's another of my favourite things.

Most days, though, I just wake up in a regular everyday kind of mood, ready for anything and those would be my *How? and Why?* days.

Nowadays you can find most things you want to know on the internet, without going anywhere, but it's not the same, because in the car we'd be talking all the time – and I'd be learning about pollution, or what a metaphor is, or where babies come from. Marian makes everything exciting and surprising and *fun*!

Marian and I spend a lot of time giggling – partners in crime, Daniel calls us, like when we make *sloppy messes in the kitchen*: papier-mâché monstrosities and plaster of Paris disasters, we call them. Our biggest project ever was the scale model we made of Mount Etna. When it was finished Marian said, conspiratorially, 'You know what we need now? An eruption!'

So we made this homemade explosive out of bicarb and vinegar. We didn't blow up the kitchen or anything dramatic like that, but there was some pretty spectacular fizzing and it certainly erupted. Mary Minchall complained for weeks afterwards about finding bits of it all over the kitchen, but Marian doesn't bother about that kind of thing; she's pretty easy going, most of the time.

For example, if I wake up feeling like having one of my *duvet-days*, I might not even bother getting dressed but instead curl up in bed all day reading.

I would have to admit that one of the things that is not ideal about our house is that it can be a bit chilly. It seems funny to me that we spend so much money heating four enormous greenhouses to keep the orchids happy, but can't afford to keep the house warmer for ourselves. Daniel doesn't seem to notice, and Marian says I should do what she does, put on more layers. And a hat, of course: usually my pink *keep-me-cosy* hat that Grandma made me, that has knitted flowers round the brim. I often cuddle up with my pet rabbit, Sir Walter Raleigh, who makes an exceptionally good hot water bottle and read *all day*! Bliss!

Marian never minds how I spend my days, as long as she knows where I am and that I'm not doing anything dangerous. Those are the only two rules, really. I must say, I think she can be a bit paranoid about me getting into danger. Like Daniel says, I'm very responsible most of the time. Even when I have my utterly mad moments I don't do *stupid* things. I've never walked out in front of a bus before!

The trouble is, since Grandma died, Marian's been different – even more of a worrier. She's been busier, because she hasn't wanted to leave Grandpa running the nursery on his own, so we've had fewer voyages of discovery. But she's had far more of her droopy days, too.

When I was little, if she had them, I'd usually stay round at Grandma and Grandpa's. But sometimes

I would choose to sit on a cushion, outside Marian's bedroom door, doing my work. Every so often she would call out, 'Hi there, munchkin, how are things on the landing? No signs of wildlife?' And I would call back, 'All quiet on the landing, Mummy. No lions and tigers,' as if I was on guard against the enemy.

Now that I'm older, I look after myself and mostly organise my own days. I've always got plenty to do and in a funny sort of way I used to feel much more on my own when I went to school than I do now. That's probably because I felt odd and different from everyone else. In my family, where we're all a bit *odd*, that feels OK. It didn't feel OK at school.

To be honest, I don't think about school most of the time. It seems far more important to other people, like Mrs Gilbert, who often brings up the subject, or the appalling Miss Morris. She makes school sound like a not very pleasant but necessary bottle of medicine.

Marian says that going to school would obviously give me some things I can't get at home, but maybe those things aren't worth what I'd have to give up – like being *me* – a quirky, brilliant, eccentric individual. (Marian's words not mine – obviously!)

I'm not sure what Grandma thought about it, she never said, but I know Grandpa's opinion, he's always argued with Marian about it.

'Chloe should be in school, with other children, not here on her own. It isn't *natural*.'

'Natural for whom, Dad?' Marian argues. 'I can't see anything natural about putting thirty or more children in a room together all day, every day, with only one adult. What's so *natural* about that?'

Grandpa shakes his head and tells Marian that if she isn't careful, she'll turn me into a solitary, introverted, little stay-at-home. (His words not mine – obviously!)

One of the things that most puts me off the idea is that, according to everything I've been told, doing well at school means knowing the right answers, whereas what Marian and Daniel have always encouraged me to do is to ask the right questions. That's as long as they're the right *kind* of questions, of course.

I've come to the conclusion that there are two kinds: safe ones – the kind you can put in the *How? and Why? Box*, that have answers that people are happy to help you search for – and unsafe ones, that never seem to get straight answers. You know, the sort of questions that make the grown-ups clear their throats, while they think how to change the subject; that make them look disappointed, or embarrassed, or make their eyes fill up with tears; the sort of questions you wish you'd never asked in the first place.

Those are questions like: *Why* does Marian disappear into her bedroom so often having droopy days? *Why* hasn't she spoken to her brother, Steve, in years? *How* is it that Grandpa and Marian both love orchids and yet seem to agree on nothing else? And *Why* do they have conversations through me, instead of talking to each other?

And when they have their arguments, which of them is right? Is Grandpa right when he says that my life isn't normal – or *natural*? Is that why I've always felt different from other kids? But what would a normal or *natural* life be like, anyway, or a normal family for that matter? I didn't really know any others to compare mine to.

Since the accident there were even more questions: *What* was this big family secret? And *Who* had they been keeping it from? *Whose* fault was it – whatever *it* was – and *Who* has had to pay for it?

So far I didn't have any of those answers. But, as Grandpa often complained, I can be like a dog with a bone sometimes, and I wasn't going to let go of this one.

Chapter Seven

A few days later, when I was getting used to being in hospital, Marian was still looking so worried about me that I began to worry about *her*.

She and Daniel were both exhausted, because whenever one of them was in the hospital with me, the other one had to be at home helping to run the nursery, and babysitting Grandpa, who had started acting very strangely. He'd been back to where I'd had the accident three times already – apparently looking for my shoe, even though they'd told him it wasn't important – and searching for his parcel, which still hadn't turned up.

'It's probably delayed shock,' Daniel said. 'Marian would like him to see a doctor, just for a check-up, but you know how stubborn Grandpa can be.'

So it was Daniel's turn to be with me. He had that

skittery look about him that he gets when he's at a particularly frustrating point with his work. He dragged his fingers through his hair while he was talking, and his eyes were flitting about. It made me feel dizzy just watching him. For weeks he'd been preparing a paper showing how far he'd got with his research, so I felt bad that he had to be there, keeping me company, instead of getting on with it.

At least the nurses were more relaxed with him around. I don't think they really knew how to handle Marian. It wasn't that they were *scared* of her, but they were definitely careful, like she was a firework that might suddenly go off. Rather than argue with her, they occasionally let her break the odd hospital rule about there being absolutely no flowers allowed on the ward. Every time Marian came in she brought an orchid with her, sometimes a *Cymbidium* or a *Cattleya*. Each time the nurses told her she had to take it home with her but at least it sat there most of the day, and only got hidden under the bed when the doctors were on the ward.

Around Daniel, though, the nurses were all smiles. I think they thought he was easier to handle than Marian – a bit less trouble. They soon changed their minds about that!

That morning we'd been trying to do some maths together. I was still feeling quite dull with the painkillers, so I wasn't up to any heavy calculations. Daniel said he'd show me some maths tricks instead.

'We'll keep it very simple,' he said, 'ones that you can easily manage in your head. Let's do something on the Magic of Nine.'

'Think of a three digit number,' Daniel told me, 'where the first and last digits are different.'

I chose 163.

'Now reverse the digits and subtract the smaller number from the larger.'

I subtracted 163 from 361 – which left 198.

'Now if you tell me either the first or the last digit,' Daniel said, 'I could give you the whole number. But before you do, I can tell you already that the middle digit is 9 and that the first and last digits will add up to 9. Am I right?'

He was! But he wasn't finished yet.

'Now, reverse the final number and add the two together...'

But before I could add 198 to 891, he said, 'I can tell you that it comes to 1089,' which it did!

'And what's more,' he said, 'whatever three digit

number you begin with, if you follow this process, you'll *always* finish with the same number – 1089.'

'Yeah, OK,' I agreed, 'that's neat.' I wanted to know why it worked but when Daniel started to explain it to me I couldn't really concentrate, so he showed me another trick instead.

When Deborah, the pretty Irish nurse, came in and saw what we were up to, she wanted to join in, and later on Gemma, too. If Jo hadn't come looking for them, I don't think there'd have been any work done for the next hour. Deborah pretended she'd actually been tidying my bed, ready for Mr Clarke's rounds. Everyone seemed to be a bit scared of Mr Clarke, and whenever he was expected they all fussed about making sure there was nothing he could find fault with.

She plumped up my pillows, which didn't need doing. 'There we are, all ready for God's representative,' she laughed. 'Now would you try and keep it that way till the man himself comes?' I nearly told her, 'I'm hardly in a position to jump out of bed and rumple it all up again, am I?'

I know I was feeling a bit crabby, already. It wasn't only my leg that was throbbing, I was still hurting all over. That morning when Jo had washed me you could see the bruising spreading right the way up my stomach.

'All the colours of the rainbow,' Jo said. 'That's quite a trophy.'

After my physiotherapy it hurt even more, so I had to have a little sleep. I don't know how long I'd slept, but when I woke up I had the weirdest sensation that Daniel was peering into my ear. He'd dragged his chair over to my bed, and his face was right up close to me. When I arched my neck to see what he was doing, there was a long line of calculations in felt pen stretching all along the white sheet.

'Daniel!' I gasped. 'What on earth will the nurses say?'

His eyes suddenly widened as if I'd woken *him* up.

'I just had this breakthrough,' he whispered. 'I could suddenly see the bit that was missing and I was afraid if I didn't write it down...'

'You could have used a notepad,' I told him.

'I did...until it ran out.' There were sheets of paper covered with figures all over the floor.

'I'm almost there,' he said, going back to his calculations.

This is the kind of thing that Daniel does. He once ruined one of Grandma's white linen tablecloths testing out a new idea that suddenly came to him.

I was wondering how he was planning to talk his way out of this with Jo, when the door opened and she put her head in. Now he's in trouble, I thought.

'Just checking you're awake. Doctor's on the ward and he's running... Ahhh!' she gasped.

She took one look at my sheet, then at Daniel who was completely away in a world of his own, then disappeared. Two minutes later she squeezed between Daniel and my bed and managed to get a clean sheet tucked half under me, the other half under the mattress, so quickly and so smoothly I thought it was better than a party trick – just as Mr Clarke and his students swept into my room.

'Delightful hat, Chloe,' he grinned. 'Always a good idea to keep the brain warm. Not bored yet, I hope?'

'*No*,' I said, firmly. I thought if anyone else asks me that question...

'Excellent. Keep up the good work,' he said, and he was out again before Daniel had even registered what was going on.

Later, when the ward rounds were finished Jo came back and set to work extracting the marked sheet from under me and replacing it with a clean one.

'The National Health Service, Mr Wells, is under

enough pressure, without patients and their relatives using hospital sheets as a notepad. If you'd asked first, I could have found you some paper.'

Daniel was falling over himself to apologise: trying to explain how he'd suddenly been seized with inspiration, but Jo wasn't impressed with Daniel's inspiration.

'We'll say no more about it this time,' she said, bundling up the ruined sheet, but Daniel didn't have the sense to leave it at that.

'I'll understand if it's not possible but...do you think I could possibly have that...?'

Jo gave him a sideways look and left.

Daniel smiled at me a bit sheepishly. 'Oh, well...' he said.

'It's OK if you want to go home, while you can still remember it all,' I told him.

'Are you sure?' he asked, looking relieved. 'Marian will be in as soon as she can.' He came over and gave me a kiss.

'Daniel, is Marian all right?' I asked, holding onto his hand. 'She's not, you know...'

'No, of course not,' he said, trying to reassure me. 'Hey, you mustn't worry about Marian. That's not going to help you get better. And I don't want to have to worry about you – worrying about Marian – worrying about you, because you know where that could lead?'

'To infinity,' I said, grinning. 'I know, but that first night in hospital, I heard Marian and Grandpa saying some very strange things.'

Daniel looked at me, suspiciously. 'What kind of things?'

'I'm not sure,' I said, 'it sort of got mixed up with my dreams, but there was something about keeping a secret…'

'What secret? Secret from whom?'

'I don't know. I'm not really sure.''

'Sounds to me like you were still dreaming,' he said. 'They'd given you enough painkillers to put a small horse to sleep.'

'I know, but…'

Daniel didn't let me finish. 'Listen, please don't worry about Marian, she'll be fine. And so will Grandpa. They're both tougher than they look you know.'

And then he was heading towards the door. As he opened it, Jo came back carrying a plastic carrier bag. She didn't say a word, in fact she looked deliberately in the opposite direction, but she handed it to Daniel, who didn't need to open it to know what was inside. This time he had the sense not to say anything.

As he left, Delia, the girl in the wheelchair, went past my door again. Daniel turned back to me and said, 'Wow! That's some hairstyle.' We both smiled. 'She might keep you company,' he suggested.

I tried to shake my head but because it still hurt so much I don't think Daniel realised and as he went out he smiled at Delia and left my door wide open, like he was inviting her in!

I tried to slide further down the bed, praying she wouldn't come in. But she did. Half fascinated, half horrified – I watched as she started to manoeuvre her wheelchair through the doorway. It took her several attempts because she kept getting stuck, and she only had one free hand because she was using the other one to keep a box of chocolates on her lap.

I kept hoping she'd give up and go away, but even though she looked as embarrassed as I was, it didn't stop her – and in the end she finally crossed the room. Even then she had to do a sort of ten-point turn to get near enough to my bed to actually offer me a chocolate. Neither of us had said a word yet, but she was smiling and holding the box almost under my nose.

'No,' I said, shaking my head as much as I could. 'Thank you very much.'

'They're *Thorntons*,' she said, surprised.

But I just shook my head again.

In the end she shrugged and turned her chair and headed back out again. I was dreading how long the whole thing was going to take in reverse, but thankfully Jo was suddenly there at the door watching us. She got behind Delia's chair and smoothly wheeled it out, back onto the ward. I was so relieved. All I could think was: what on earth would we have talked about?

Later on, when Jo came back to do my checks, she asked me, 'Now what was that all about?'

'What do you mean?' I said.

'You know what I mean: that business with Delia?'

I shrugged. 'I just didn't want a chocolate.'

'It was nothing to do with *chocolates*,' Jo said, smiling, but sounding quite exasperated with me. 'Delia was trying to be friendly. That's how it works, Chloe.'

I think I must have gone red, because I was suddenly feeling very hot.

'Do you have many friends?' she asked.

'No, not really,' I admitted. 'I don't go to school, you see.'

'I know that, but what about at home?' I shook my head.

Jo smiled at me. 'Don't you ever get lonely?'

I thought, here we go again. Why do people always assume that someone on their own can't be happy?

'I think if you keep yourself busy and your brain occupied,' I told her, 'there's always something to do. I don't usually have time to get bored.'

Jo was looking at me like she could suddenly see inside my head. 'Nobody said anything about boredom, child,' she said. 'That's a different kettle of fish, altogether.'

Well, I wasn't sure I could see the difference, and I always hate people calling me a *child*. I was feeling tired again anyway and I didn't want to talk any more, so just I closed my eyes, but Jo suddenly got hold of my hand and stroked it, which I wasn't expecting.

'You get some rest, Chloe. I'll see you tomorrow, and God keep you safe till then.'

'I don't believe in God,' I said. I didn't mean it to come out sounding snappy, but I knew it had.

Jo looked at me surprised, but she didn't say anything.

I started to explain, 'I think...that is, *we* all think, you can't believe in something, unless it can be proved. Like in maths,' I said, 'until it's proved it's just a conjecture – that's like a theory, you know...'

'Yes, Chloe,' she interrupted me, 'I know very well what it is, but here's my theory: I can't prove to you there is a God, and you can't prove to me there isn't, but I know which makes me happier.' She squeezed my hand again.

I looked down at Jo's much larger black hand, her skin almost shiny against mine, and it was suddenly so hard not to cry. I was determined I wouldn't, though, not until Jo had gone. I closed my eyes again instead.

I kept wishing Marian would come in soon. I was missing her and Daniel and Grandpa and The Log. I suddenly felt really *alone*, which isn't exactly the same as being *lonely*, at least I don't think it is.

Chapter Eight

Friends with Numbers

FRIENDLY NUMBERS are sometimes called AMICABLE
PAIRS, which are sort of related to PERFECT
NUMBERS.
220 and 284 are called friendly numbers because
220 is the sum of the factors of 284 — which means
the sum of the numbers it is exactly divisible by:
1 + 2 + 4 + 71 + 142
And 284 is the sum of the factors of 220:
1 + 2 + 4 + 5 + 10 + 11 + 20 + 22 + 44 + 55 + 110
There seem to be as few friendly numbers as
there are perfect numbers.
At least very few have been discovered — so far.

A long time ago, when friendly numbers were first
discovered, people believed that they were symbolic
of friendship. They might engrave them on two pieces
of jewellery, wear one, with 220 on it, and give the
other, with 284 on it, to their best friend.

After Daniel told me that story, I made matching

pendants for him and Marian – out of cardboard and felt pen – because he and Marian are my best friends. Come to think of it, I'm probably their best friend too. Marian says we're like a team, the three of us. I suppose that's partly why I call them Marian and Daniel, instead of Mum and Dad. It was one of those things that started when I was six or seven and it sort of stuck.

To be honest, we're not a family that goes in for lots of friends – apart from Grandma. She was really good at making friends.

Grandma and Grandpa have lived here on the edge of the village for fifteen years, ever since Grandpa left the army. When they first came to Norfolk, partly because they had lived in so many different countries, and partly because Grandma had not been well for a while, they both said they didn't want to travel anywhere else, *ever again*.

Well, Grandma got her wish, because she died last year and now she's buried in the churchyard in the village. Lots of people came to her funeral.

Grandma made friends wherever she went: shopping, to the library, at the Gardening Club, the WI – or at church. Grandma didn't agree with Marian and Daniel about God. She said that on such an important and personal subject people should decide for themselves and she said I should keep an open mind, until I was older.

Grandma thought it was important for me to have friends too and she tried really hard to make it happen, first of all with Mary's granddaughter, Hayley.

As well as being her cleaner, Mary was Grandma's friend. They would often spend more time chatting, or swopping recipes and plants for the garden, than Mary spent actually cleaning. Mary's granddaughter used to stay with Mary in the holidays and once or twice Mary persuaded Hayley to play with me. It didn't work out very well, because basically we had nothing in common. Marian said that was because Hayley wasn't very bright and had a head full of nonsense, but actually she *was* bright; she knew about all sorts of things I didn't. In fact she often told me that I was the stupid one.

'How can you *not* know about *Big Brother*?' she laughed. 'That's ridiculous!'

When I asked Daniel who Big Brother was, he said it was a character in a book called *1984* by *George Orwell*. He said the book was probably a bit old for me, but he'd got a copy if I wanted to try it. I found it very interesting, actually, but when I tried to talk to Hayley about it afterwards, she looked at me as if I'd just arrived from another planet.

'It's not in a stupid *book*! It's a reality programme – on *TV*!' she said. 'Don't you know anything? Honestly, you're weird. I think you're a bit daft in the head.'

I realise there are lots of things that I don't know. A person's head can only hold so much and Marian says you have to choose. I like to watch a bit of TV – documentaries, sometimes, and wildlife programmes – you can learn a lot from those, but Marian and Daniel don't like me to watch too much. They'd rather I read. Hayley said reading was boring.

Another time Grandma tried to introduce me to the vicar's son, the disgusting Duncan. He's a year older than me and he's away at boarding school in term time. The first time he came to my house wasn't too bad, but the second time he started being horrible and saying what a good job it was that I didn't go to his school, because they'd probably eat me alive. Whenever he said anything that I didn't exactly understand, and I asked, 'What does that mean?' he did a funny waving thing with his finger against the side of his head.

'Durr! What do you think it means?! Nutty, crackers, loony, barmy.'

I wasn't sure I knew what any of those things meant exactly either, but I could tell they weren't very nice. When I told Grandma, she apologised and said it had been a bad idea in the first place and she should never have suggested it.

'He was obviously a very silly boy,' she said. 'Forget about him.'

I was just glad I didn't have to see him again. Unfortunately it still didn't stop Grandma – and Grandpa – trying to introduce me to any other children who visited the nursery with their parents. One or other of them would say, 'Chloe would you like to show Paul...or Jane...or Jeremy...round the orchid houses?' And I'd think: *if I have to*, and they'd look like they were thinking: *do we have to*?

I'd try to make it interesting, like Grandpa does, telling them stories: like the one about the *Star of Bethlehem* orchid that relies on one particular moth to pollinate it. This orchid stores its nectar so deep inside the flower that the moth that pollinates it has had to evolve a tongue *thirty centimetres long* to reach it. Do you realise how long that is? It's the length of a ruler!

That's *amazing*. But they didn't seem to think so, their eyes would glaze over, or they'd yawn as if I was boring them to death. I could see they thought I was weird as well.

Now, whenever I notice any children around I usually disappear. Not completely, because I quite like watching them, but I try not to get into conversation with them. It feels too difficult. I'd rather do a maths problem any day.

I don't blame Grandma; I know she was trying to be kind. She was always kind; she even had kind eyes. When Marian had droopy days, or if she was just too busy with work, Grandma was always happy to let me join in with whatever she was doing: baking or gardening, or sometimes we'd just snuggle together on the sofa. She was the one who bought me dolls, and made clothes for them, and taught me to knit, and skip, and roller-skate. She was the one who taught me to swim too, although I didn't get to be all that good at it.

That was the only time I ever saw Grandma really lose her temper with Marian. When it was first suggested that we go swimming, Marian had one of her funny turns. She looked like she might suddenly break out screaming, although she never actually does. She just takes a deep breath in and forgets to breathe out.

But Grandma said, 'Now, listen to me Marian. This is important for Chloe and I am determined to take her whether you like it or not.'

Marian tried arguing, but Grandpa joined in and settled it. 'It's your problem, Marian, not Chloe's, and you're just going to have to get your head round it.'

Marian didn't like it, but she must have got her head round it, because we went most Mondays for about six months, until Grandma got properly sick, then lots of things stopped – like the piano lessons.

Grandma and I used to play together most days after lunch: duets and comic songs that made us giggle. Before she got ill, Grandma was always laughing, especially at Grandpa. She called him the original grumpy old man, although he wasn't as grumpy then, when she was alive. I don't know what she'd think if she could see him now.

Grandma liked orchids, but she didn't love them, like Grandpa does. She said she was an orchid widow and I was an orchid orphan, but at least we had each other.

'There's nothing sadder, Chloe,' she told me, 'than an old man who talks to flowers and a young woman who spends her days pollinating them with a toothpick. Don't you fall under the spell of orchids; it's a hard habit to break.'

What Grandma *did* really love, though, were celebrations: Christmas and Easter and Bonfire Night and spooky stories at Halloween. She always made those times special. She told me, after she got ill, 'Rituals are very important, Chloe, and don't you let them forget that.'

A few weeks after Grandma died, I collected together a lot of things that made me think of her: like my first doll, Annabelle, and the little mini knitting needles she'd taught me to knit on, and the fan she'd once bought in Bali, and some bits of jewellery she gave me. I put them into one of Grandpa's cigar-boxes. I was going to bury it and have a little ritual ceremony on my own, because I thought Grandma's funeral was quite miserable – not a bit like she would have chosen, if anyone had asked her what she wanted.

When it came to it, though, I couldn't bear to bury any of the things she'd given me, so I wrapped the box in a plastic bag instead and hid it inside a hollow part of The Log. I sang some of the songs she used to like and made up a poem and sort of said my own goodbye to her. But actually I often go and sit out there, on The Log, and talk to Grandma, so it didn't really feel like goodbye.

My memories of her seem to have got a bit mixed up now. Mostly I remember her as kind and smiley and happy, but there were times when we were together that she looked quite sad and those are the times I keep remembering.

I think Grandma sometimes felt a bit sorry for me, because she would squeeze me to her and say, 'Oh, Chloe, Chloe, Chloe...' except that there was this one time, when I'd fallen off the swing and skinned my knee, and Grandma hugged me and stroked my head and said, 'Oh, Libby, Libby, Libby...' and I was so surprised that I stopped feeling sorry for myself and asked, 'Who's Libby, Grandma?'

Grandma's face looked really anxious, but she tried to make a joke of it.

'It was nothing, my dear girl, just your Grandma getting old and confused. Sometimes I could forget my own name.' And she immediately got up and said, 'Homemade blackberry ice cream – that's the perfect thing for poorly knees.'

Later she said to me, 'Let's not mention that silly mistake of mine to your mummy. You know how she worries about everything. Our little secret, eh?'

I never did say anything to Marian or Daniel about it. Grandma and I often shared secrets, nothing major, just about her giving me extra sweets when Marian and Daniel didn't really approve, or her telling me what she was giving the others for Christmas or for their birthdays. Grandma knew she could trust me, because I'm excellent at keeping secrets.

Those weren't *proper* secrets, though, just surprises, like everyone likes to keep. But I could tell from the way Marian and Grandpa had been arguing in the hospital that this wasn't the kind of secret they'd been talking about. This was something much more serious and it was starting to bother me – a bit like a sore spot in your mouth that you can't keep your tongue away from. It was bothering me because I felt sure it had something to do with me.

Having someone to share secrets and surprises with was just another reason why I wished Grandma hadn't died, and why I missed her.

I suppose you can have secrets that you keep just to yourself – little things that you don't really want to tell anyone else in case they don't come true, maybe – like dreams and ambitions.

One of mine – and I haven't even told Daniel this – is to discover something new in mathematics. For example, for a long time there were very few *friendly numbers* known about, but, in the nineteenth century, an Italian boy, not so very much older than me, discovered a completely new pair: 1,184 and 1,210. He became famous throughout the world.

Daniel told me that lots of important mathematical discoveries have been made by quite young people. He says that in maths, experience isn't everything; sometimes it's about being young and daring and full of ambition.

I would love to think that in the future people would say, 'In the twenty-first century an English girl called Chloe Wells discovered a new *prime number*... or a new *perfect number*.' That would be so exciting!

I know it's not the same as having real friends, but I feel as if numbers are like my friends, always there to play with. OK, that sounds pretty weird, doesn't it? Just forget I ever said it.

Chapter Nine

There were so many different things to get used to in hospital and one of the strangest so far had been having my hair washed lying down in bed!

Usually, if my fringe needs trimming, Marian does it, but there was one birthday when Grandma took me to the hairdresser's as a treat. We sat, side by side, having our hair washed in those backward basins, so I know what that feels like, but this time I was almost flat on my back with my leg still strapped up in the air. It wasn't easy but you could tell Jo had done it lots of times before.

'However, it would be a whole lot easier if you didn't have *quite* so much hair,' she told me.

'You can cut it off if you like,' I told her. 'I'm not that attached to it.'

'I was joking, Chloe. You've got beautiful hair. You mustn't think of cutting it off.'

Grandma used to say that too, but Marian thinks long hair is more trouble than it's worth. The fact is, though, if you tie it back in a ponytail like I do, long hair is just as easy as short, apart from the time it takes to dry.

Since Jo and I had had that argument about God I'd been feeling a little awkward around her, but she must have forgotten all about it, because she was still being very nice to me. In fact while she dried my hair she sang to me, which reminded me of Grandma and almost made me cry.

It was always very hot in my room, but I was starting to think that there might be something else about the air in hospitals that made everyone feel bored, because even I was beginning to feel it.

There were lots of things I could have done, but I couldn't be bothered with any of them. I was glad it was taking Jo so long to dry my hair. I wanted her to stay all day, singing to me and telling me about the other children on the ward.

Most of the ones my age were in and out in a couple of days, Jo said, as I would have been if mine had been a simple fracture. Some, like me, weren't allowed, or able, to get out of bed. But Jo reminded me that there was always Delia, who was around my age – if I was looking for a bit of company!

She didn't say any more than that, but I could feel her eyes on me. They were a bit laser-like, Jo's eyes, and I felt there wasn't much they couldn't discover if you made the mistake of looking back into them, so I looked away. But she'd set me off thinking that maybe I didn't have to spend the next four weeks entirely on my own – feeling bored.

Possibly, and it was only a tiny possibility, I might be able to make friends with Delia. She'd seemed nice, when she offered me a chocolate, not like the horrible Hayley or the disgusting Duncan; perhaps it would be different with her. Anyway, what was the worst she could say – that she thought I was weird? It wouldn't be the first time. I started to dare myself to do it.

But a couple of days later I was still trying to work up the courage.

It was Daniel's turn to be with me, because Marian was finally taking Grandpa to see the doctor. Grandpa was still being stubborn about it, but Marian can be just as stubborn when she puts her mind to it.

Daniel was sitting silently in the corner, staring into

space. Really, he might as well not have been there. Apparently when he'd got home the other day and checked out the equations he'd written on my sheet, he'd found that the whole calculation had been flawed, which meant it was back to square one again, or as Marian sometimes joked, back to the attic, which is where Daniel has his study.

I was hiding behind a book, not really reading, instead trying to hatch a plan. I was thinking that there must be a way of doing this. I'm good at problem-solving, after all.

When I was younger, Daniel taught me different strategies like – *Computing and Simplifying*, *Using a Formula*, or *Making Charts*, or *Tables*. But I couldn't see how any of those might help here. There was one I remembered, though, which I'd never really been able to use on my own. It was called *Acting out the Problem*. Imagine this question: There are ten people invited to a party. The host has to introduce each person to every one else at the party. How many introductions will she have to make?

The idea is that you could act out that problem, if you had ten friends, which I can't quite imagine, or more likely if there were that many people in your class at school. Each person would pretend to be one of the guests.

With a problem like that, I would always have made a chart or a table instead, but maybe this new problem was one that I *could* act out – inside my head, at least. I closed my eyes and tried to imagine what I might do next time Delia passed my door. First I might wave to catch her attention, then I'd say, 'Hi, Delia!'

OK, so far, so good. What next?

I needed a way to get her into the room. She'd offered me a chocolate, maybe I could offer her...some of Marian's homemade flapjack? Probably not. I don't mind it, but it's what Grandpa calls an acquired taste – heavy on the oats and light on the sugar. Still, looking at it logically, Delia wouldn't know Marian's flapjacks aren't as good as Thorntons chocolates, until she'd tasted one. By then I'd have got her in the room and I could start up a conversation – but what conversation? It still came back to the root of the problem – *whatever would we talk about*?

If I'd been at all tempted to ask Daniel's advice, one look in his direction would have told me not to bother. In fact, I realised that if I stood any chance of doing this I had to get rid of him, I'd never pull it off with an audience.

'I'm feeling really tired,' I told Daniel (which was half the truth), 'I might have a little nap. I'm OK if you want to go home...'

Daniel didn't need much persuading. He promised me that Marian would be in later. After he'd gone I spent the next hour watching the clock – I knew that Delia came back from school around three. By then I was *so* nervous that the moment I heard her wheelchair coming, I started madly waving one arm. It was a good job I did because my voice turned into a sort of little mouse squeak that she would never have heard.

Delia must have thought I was in some sort of trouble because she called out, 'Nurse! Nurse! Quick!'

Deborah hurried in but after I'd explained that there was nothing actually wrong, she went back to the ward. I held out the box of flapjack to Delia and the strategy worked. She came in and actually took a piece!

'Thanks,' she said. 'What is it?' I thought she was pretty brave, taking it without knowing, but, like Jo said, it wasn't about flapjack.

I really needn't have worried; we seemed to find plenty to talk about.

'I've just got back from school,' Delia started.

I nodded, because I knew that. 'What's it like?' I asked.

She wrinkled up her nose. 'Better than my regular school, but it's still school, you know. You still have to work.'

There were a few awkward silences like when Delia asked me, 'Where do you go to school?' and I said, 'I don't go to school,' and she said, 'Yeah, right,' and laughed. I didn't know what to say to that.

'How come you have a room of your own?' she asked me.

'Marian had an argument with the nurses,' I said, 'and she won.'

'Who's Marian?' Delia asked.

I said, 'My mum,' so she said, 'Well, why don't you call her that?' but it just seemed too difficult to explain, so I shrugged and smiled.

I think Delia was finding the flapjack more than a bit chewy, although she was trying to hide the fact, so I said, 'It's not very good is it, not if you want to hold onto your teeth?' and she grinned and I showed her where the bin was.

After that we seemed to get along really well.

When Delia asked what had happened to me, I told her all about my accident and about my shattered femur. I think I might have given her a bit too much detail, which is something I know I have a tendency to do, and I probably shouldn't have lifted my pyjama top and shown her the bruising which was right up to my waist by then, because she looked a bit sick and said, 'Oh, gross. Too much information, put it away.'

I didn't like to ask her exactly why she was in a wheelchair, but she told me anyway. She'd been at her dance class and somehow twisted her knee.

'That's all I did,' she said. 'No big deal, but something sort of popped out and it's never been right since. Look, I still can't straighten this leg and I've had a couple of operations on it.'

She told me she'd had hours of physio, too, and hydrotherapy. She'd been on the ward for two months already. But when I asked her exactly what was still wrong with her knee, she didn't seem very clear.

'So how much longer are you likely to be here?' I asked, but she didn't seem to know that either.

'Nobody tells *me* anything,' she complained.

'I suppose until I'm out of this wheelchair and using crutches.'

'And how long will that take?'

She rolled her eyes and said, 'You ask an awful lot of questions, don't you?'

'Oh, I know, I'm sorry,' I said. 'Grandpa's always telling me that. I'm just naturally curious, I guess.'

'Well, you know what happened to the cat?' she grinned.

'He wasn't the one that got the cream, was he?' I said, and she burst out laughing, which made things feel a bit better.

After a while she said, 'Seriously, though, where *do* you go to school?'

'Seriously, I don't.'

'Everyone *has* to go to school,' she insisted.

'They don't,' I said. 'It's not against the law, as long as someone teaches you at home.' I could see she still didn't believe me. 'I did go for a while, when I was five,' I told her. 'I just didn't settle. I think I was a bit scared.'

'Yeah, I had a horrid teacher once.'

'No, it was the other kids,' I said, which she seemed to think was hilarious.

'You are funny,' she said, giggling, and I thought,

here we go, I've done it now, she thinks I'm weird. I wished I hadn't said any of that.

My face must have dropped, because Delia quickly explained, 'No, I meant funny, ha, ha. You really make me laugh.'

I was surprised because I've never been any good at telling jokes and I'm just as bad at getting them, unless they're puns – you know, plays on words.

Grandpa gets cross when he has to explain jokes to me. He says, 'It rather defeats the object, Chloe!'

'That hat's a scream,' Delia suddenly said. 'Can I try it on?'

I was wearing my green felt one, which is covered with brooches and badges. I handed it to her even though I could see she'd never get it over her hair. It sat perched on top like one of those mini party hats.

'You think *I'm* funny,' I giggled, 'you should see yourself right now.'

Delia said, 'You cheeky mare,' which I didn't understand, because a mare's a female horse, isn't it? But it sounded so funny I started giggling again, and then so did Delia. After that we couldn't stop. We must have been making so much noise that Jo put her head round the door. Her eyes went as big as saucers, but she didn't say anything. She just went away smiling.

'It's not that I've got a big head,' Delia insisted, giving me back my hat.

'I wouldn't have dared suggest such a thing,' I said, and she laughed again.

'It's because I've got so much hair.'

I told her I thought her hair was absolutely *beauteous*.

Delia frowned and said, 'I think you mean beautiful.'

I said, 'It probably means the same thing but it sounds more special, more magical – to me anyway.' Then I went a bit pink because she was looking at me like that was...you know...a pretty weird thing to say.

But she shrugged and said, 'I could do a few corn rows for you if you like.'

I'd never heard the words before, but I guessed she must have been talking about the hundreds of tiny plaits she had all over her head.

'OK,' I said, really excited, although it wasn't going to be easy with me laid up in bed and her in a wheelchair. Every time she tried to get close enough, she kept bumping into the bed.

'Oh, sorry, sorry, sorry,' she said, and then did exactly the same all over again. In the end I didn't even wince any more because we were laughing so much instead.

Finally Delia got close enough to reach my hair. It felt weird then; to have someone I'd only just met actually touching my hair. Apart from my family, no one else ever does that. But even though it felt scary, it felt OK as well.

'Your hair's so different to mine,' Delia said. 'Soft and fine. Mine's thick and crinkly, a bit like me probably.'

I didn't like Delia saying that about herself. She didn't seem in the least bit thick to me.

She said, 'Jo says you're a real brain-box.'

I was a bit surprised and wondered what else Jo had told her about me.

'Oh, yes,' I said, trying to make a joke of it. 'I'm a regular Einstein,' which is something Grandpa calls me when I'm getting on his nerves.

'What's that?' she asked me – with a completely straight face, which really made me laugh.

'*He* is only the cleverest man who ever lived,' I said.

'Durr,' she said, pulling a silly face. 'See what I mean?'

And then we were both laughing again. That's probably why we didn't notice Marian come into the room. Delia saw her first and stopped plaiting my hair. When I caught Marian's face it was full of surprise, shock even, as if she'd caught us doing something wrong. Delia saw it too and she quickly undid the plaits and tried to smooth them out.

'Marian, this is Delia,' I said. 'Delia, this is my mum.'

Even though she looked quite awkward Delia smiled and said, 'Hi.' Marian nodded and smiled back, but she didn't say anything to Delia; she turned to me instead and told me how tired I was looking. 'Have you had a nap yet?'

'No,' I said, 'I didn't need one.'

'You do if you ever plan to get better,' she said. 'Maybe it would be a good idea if Delia came back some other time.'

I said again that I was fine, but Marian kept on until I could see just why the nurses had given up the fight so easily. I hadn't often seen this side of Marian and I didn't really like it. She was a bit like a different person since my accident.

Jo came in then and must have caught the end of the conversation. As she helped Delia through the doorway, she said, 'Maybe you two could get together later on and watch a bit of TV?'

'Yeah, great!' Delia said. 'We could watch *Corrie*

in here. It'd be much cooler than watching it on the ward.'

I smiled and nodded. I had no idea what *Corrie* was but it didn't matter.

'See you later, then,' Delia said, waving.

I noticed Jo and Marian exchange looks, but neither said anything.

After they'd gone Marian said to me, 'You don't have to let anyone come in here you know, if you don't want them to.'

'I know,' I said, smiling. 'But Delia seems nice.'

'Yes, well, you've said that before, sweetheart,' Marian reminded me, 'and look where it's usually ended – in tears.' She squeezed my hand. 'Anyway now you've got a door you can keep it closed. In fact maybe I should tell Jo that.'

I didn't argue with Marian, even though I wanted to, and she launched then into a long story about how impossible Grandpa had been with the doctor. I didn't listen properly, because I was thinking about what Marian had just said. I didn't want her to bring up all the other times I'd tried to make friends and it hadn't worked. Why couldn't she have just been a little bit more pleased for me that I'd even tried?

Grandma would have been hanging out the flags and inviting Delia to tea.

Marian kept on about Grandpa completely obsessing about his lost parcel. 'I know perfectly well what was in it – orchid bulbs, but he won't admit it. I suppose they're ones he got on the internet. He's definitely heading for trouble,' she grumbled on.

But I still wasn't really listening. If I was as hopeless at making friends as everyone said I was, why wasn't she trying to help, instead of scaring Delia off by behaving like some bad-tempered woman? This wasn't how Marian usually behaved. What on earth was wrong with her?

I suddenly tuned back into what she was saying when she started to grumble that lately Grandpa had been even more *secretive* than usual.

It reminded me that I still hadn't tackled Marian about the secret I'd overheard her and Grandpa arguing about. I was just going to ask when the lady with the tea trolley opened the door and came in with my food.

'Macaroni cheese, just what the doctor ordered,' she said.

After that the nurses were in and out doing checks

and later Daniel came back and I'd missed my chance, but I was determined to find another one.

Until now, I hadn't really thought much about the fact that Marian and Daniel had never tried to push me into making friends in the way that Grandma and Grandpa had. I'd assumed it was because I wasn't very good at it – which is what everyone always said – and that they were trying to protect my feelings. But now Marian actually seemed determined to keep me away from Delia.

Well, it was too late. I'd already discovered that talking to Delia hadn't felt weird or scary or difficult. I'd been pretty good at it. It had felt quite...*ordinary*.

In fact, as soon as Marian went home, I was going to do it again.

Chapter Ten

Not Exactly Perfect

There are very few PERFECT NUMBERS.
Most numbers are either EXCESSIVE NUMBERS, which means that their factors add up to more than the number itself, for example:
12, whose factors 1...2...3...4...6 add up to 16
or DEFECTIVE NUMBERS which means that their factors add up to less than the number itself, for example: 10 whose factors 1...2...5 add up to 8.
But there are some numbers whose factors add up to only one less than the number itself, for example 8 (1 + 2 + 4 = 7) and these are called SLIGHTLY DEFECTIVE NUMBERS.
Interestingly, there are no SLIGHTLY EXCESSIVE NUMBERS. At least no one has discovered any yet!

Personally, I've always felt a bit sorry for *defective numbers*. They sound like they don't work properly. *excessive numbers* sound as if they've been over-eating and only have themselves to blame. And *slightly defective numbers* still aren't perfect, are they, which is what everyone really wants to be?

I suppose I've always been a bit soft in that way. I've never liked to think of anyone, or anything, being looked down on, or rejected, or having to suffer, which is partly why I'm a vegetarian, I suppose.

It's the same with stories. I hate it when anyone gets hurt. It's not that I'm normally someone who cries easily, like when I used to climb trees and fell and hurt myself, or had to have an injection, or even when I had my accident. But sad stories always make me reach for a hanky.

The first time I watched a video was with Grandma. It was the one about Winnie the Pooh and the Honey Bees, you know, where Pooh floats up in the air holding onto balloons hoping to steal the bees' honey, but the bees spot him and start buzzing all round him. Well, apparently, I burst into tears and begged Grandma to rescue him. I thought the bees were going to sting Pooh and he'd let go of the balloons, fall to the ground and get killed! I was so upset that Grandma had to switch it off and promise to find a way of getting Pooh safely down to earth, which of course is what happens in the video, if only I'd been patient and waited.

So, later, when Grandma showed me how Christopher Robin comes along with his gun and shoots the balloons, which slowly deflate and bring Pooh safely down to earth, I naturally believed it was Grandma that had made it all right.

After that, whenever I saw a film or read a book where something sad or tragic happened, we had to stop until Grandma worked out exactly how we were going to save the person and get them out of trouble.

It's always been a family joke that books and films had to have a *Chloe-rating* depending on how sad, or how tragic, they were. *A Dog so Small* was a three-hanky read and so was *Charlotte's Web*. When Wilbur loses his best friend Charlotte it nearly broke my heart. I begged Marian to write to the author and ask him to bring her back to life in his next book, but she told me that E.B. White had already died and wouldn't be writing any more books anyway.

When I was a bit older Grandma sat me down and said, 'Look, Chloe, you're very soft-hearted, and there's nothing wrong with that, but you have to realise that if you were to take *all* the sad bits – all the tragedy and the conflict – out of books, there wouldn't be anything much left for writers to write about. Those are the bits that make great stories, and if you want to go on to read wonderful books like *Little Women* and *Black Beauty* and *Jane Eyre*, you're going to have to get used to the fact that in stories, like in life, people have accidents, get ill, and sometimes even die.'

As I got older, I still didn't like it, but I found a way of having my stories *and* eating them, so to speak. What I did – in fact what I sometimes still do with sad stories – was to make up my own versions and find ways to rescue everyone and sort out their problems. I call it *de-tragifying* – which probably isn't a real word, but it works for me and, if I say so myself, I'm pretty good at it. I think it would be better if writers did a bit more of it, too. If I were a writer I'd make sure that tragedy was *always* averted. Nobody would die in my stories!

I suppose making up stories, and *de-tragifying* them, is a bit like playing at being god – getting to change everyone's fate. Not like being *God*, because, as if I've told you before, I don't believe in *him*, but more like one of the Greek gods, handing out wisdom and justice. Not a harsh, cruel, big bully like Zeus, but perhaps Apollo, a more kind-hearted god. And the place I always go to play at being god is The Log.

My garden at home is quite long and in two halves. The top half, near the house, has a few flowerbeds and a sandpit and a swing, and a few vegetables growing, but then you take a sharp turn, past a derelict old greenhouse, which Daniel is always going to do up, but never does, through a gate and then you come into an orchard, completely out of sight of the house. There are dozens of old fruit trees and tucked away at the very bottom is The Log.

A *log* doesn't really describe it, to be honest. It's the whole trunk of an ancient apple tree that came down in the storms of 1987. Do you know, there were fifteen *million* trees blown down in one night, whole forests lost, winds of 120 miles per hour recorded on the Norfolk coast? It was the worst damage in Britain in 300 years and, strictly speaking, it wasn't even a hurricane, it was only a storm!

Uh-oh. See what I mean about a head full of stuff?

Well, anyway that's how we got The Log and it was agreed in the family that it's my domain. Grandpa and Daniel carved out a huge seat for me, like a throne where, when I was little, I used to dress up and pretend to be Queen of the Log. Now it's where I go to play god and do a bit of *de-tragifying*.

In my *de-tragified* versions of stories there are no deaths or disasters, no tears or tragedies, no doom and gloom. But I'd have to admit that Grandma was right, it isn't always easy to do, because once you start to take out the sad or tragic bits, the whole story has a tendency to fall apart, like a piece of knitting coming off the needles.

I absolutely worshipped *Little Women* when I first read it, although it does have a lot of doom and gloom in it, and it wasn't easy to take it out. For example, if Mr March didn't ever go off to the war, then the family would never have been so poor and wouldn't have been befriended by Mr Laurence and Laurie, which wouldn't leave much of a story, would it? So I decided that I'd have to let him go, even though normally in my stories I'd never allow any wars!

But in *Good Wives*, the second book, I simply, utterly could not bear how sad it was. I wouldn't have let Laurie waste his time studying *art* in Europe, in fact I made him become a doctor and discover a cure for Beth's illness and go home and marry her instead. If anyone *had* to die, then I would make it someone old like Aunt March or Mr Laurence!

I'd been reading *Jane Eyre* since my accident and

that has to be one of the most tragic stories I've ever read. That was going to take a lot of *de-tragifying* when I finally got home to The Log.

After Grandma died, and everyone else was so much busier, and since I'd fallen out with Grandpa, I'd spent a lot more time on The Log. I'd attempted, once or twice, to *de-tragify* my own story.

In my version of things Grandma never got ill and didn't die; Grandpa didn't get to be so grumpy; the doctor found a cure for Marian's droopy days, and Daniel didn't disappear into his study until he sometimes forgot what day it was. In fact all the grown-ups, instead of being quiet and sad so much of the time, were more like their old selves.

Since Grandma died, it wasn't that my life was bad exactly; it just wasn't *exactly perfect*.

I'm not stupid; I know that you can't turn the clock back and change things that have already happened, like Grandma dying. You can't even change stories – except in your own head. And I know that life can't always be perfect. But I suppose I just kept on hoping that things might get back to how they were – not exactly the same, of course, because there would always be a hole where Grandma used to be.

When I read sad stories, I don't get quite so upset nowadays. I'm not sure if that's because I'm getting older, or if it means that I'm not quite as soft-hearted as I used to be, but I think deep down I'll always be a person who prefers their stories to have happy endings, and like Grandma said, there's nothing wrong with that.

Chapter Eleven

I don't really know how it happened, but Delia fell out with me. And just when things had been going really well. It was probably my fault.

We'd been spending lots of time together, watching TV – I found out what *Corrie* is: a TV programme, called *Coronation Street*, which is Delia's favourite thing. We'd also been listening to music – all Delia's favourite groups.

Each day, after school, after she'd finished her physio, Delia came to my room and I helped her with her homework. I found it pretty easy, which just confirmed Delia's idea that I was some kind of brain-box. And then once that was out of the way we'd just hang out – that's what Delia called it.

I still couldn't understand why Marian didn't like the idea, because it meant that she and Daniel didn't have to spend quite so much time in the hospital with me. She was still looking so tense that the bags under her eyes looked more like suitcases.

Of course, I knew that Marian wasn't only worrying about me, she was worrying about Grandpa too. He'd been to visit me in the hospital a couple of times and I was shocked to see how old he was suddenly looking. In fact, he came to visit me on the day that I had the fall out with Delia.

He sat for ages holding my hand, which cheered me up, because I'd been thinking that he'd gone off me.

'It's very quiet around the nursery without you,' he said. 'Everyone's missing you – especially me.'

When he started talking about my accident, he cried, which was horrible.

'Don't get upset, Grandpa,' I said. 'I'm getting better. I'll soon be back pestering the life out of you, asking too many questions.' But even that didn't make him smile; he just squeezed my hand. 'Did you find your parcel of orchids?' I asked him, but he just frowned and shook his head.

'They're more trouble than they're worth,' he grumbled. 'If it hadn't been for that parcel, I'd never have been there in the village, you wouldn't have run out in front of the bus and none of this would have happened.'

'It was my own silly fault for running out without looking,' I told him. 'Nobody blames you, Grandpa.'

'I think your mother does, when she's not blaming herself.'

'Have you two been arguing again?' I asked.

'I don't argue with anybody,' he insisted. 'It's her that argues with me.'

'Only because she thinks you keep things from her,' I said. 'You know, secrets and things?' I was trying to gently lead the conversation round, but he suddenly got cross.

'Me?! That's rich, that is. She's the one with secrets!' And then he went quiet and looked out of the window.

'Grandpa...' I tried again, more carefully. 'You know that first night when I was in hospital...'

Grandpa looked at me, narrowing his eyes, and said, quite sharply, 'You're not going to start plaguing me with more of your questions, are you? Not now. You just concentrate on getting better.'

'I was only going to ask you about something you said to Marian...'

'Well, don't!' he said, firmly, cutting me off. 'I'm in enough trouble with your mother already. Don't you make matters any worse.'

'But Marian doesn't have to know...' I tried again. 'I won't tell her.'

'What have I told you about a dog and a bone? Now, let it go.'

I sighed and gave up. In Grandpa's present mood there was no point asking again. He was being so nice one minute, then as bad-tempered as ever the next. No wonder Marian and Daniel were worried about him.

I'd been in quite a lot of pain that day because they'd started to reduce my painkillers. I hadn't told Jo at first, but later when I did, she said I should have asked earlier.

'You don't have to put on a brave face all the time,' she said. 'A bit of pain is inevitable, but you have to tell us when it's too much.'

Funnily enough, that was what Delia and I ended up falling out about: being in pain and what to do about it – that and the thing that Grandpa had been telling me off for: not being able to leave things alone. Dogs and bones!

After her physio session, Delia came into my room

in a really bad mood. I asked her what was wrong, and she wouldn't say. But you know me.

'Well, you don't look very happy,' I kept on, stating the obvious.

'I'm sick of those exercises. I'm not going to do them any more.'

'But if you don't do them, you won't get better,' I told her.

'I'm not getting better anyway,' she snapped.

'You probably are,' I said. 'It just takes a long time.'

'Well, it hurts too much,' she said and her eyes filled up.

'Have you told the physio that?'

'Of course!' she snapped again. 'She just says it will hurt a bit, but I've got to put up with that to get the knee moving.'

'Maybe she's right,' I said. So then Delia asked whose side I was on, and I said, surely it wasn't about sides.

'Sometimes things get worse before they get better,' I told her. 'When I'm doing really difficult calculations and suddenly I get in a muddle, I don't want to have to go right back to the beginning and start all over again, but I know I have to and that can feel pretty painful.'

Delia sat staring at me, like she couldn't believe what she was hearing. That was the point at which I should have stopped, but I just kept digging anyway.

'When my leg hurts me,' I told her, 'I try to think about other things. I pretend I'm somewhere else, like at home on The Log. Perhaps if you had somewhere like that to imagine, then it wouldn't hurt so much.'

Delia still didn't say anything, but she turned her face away from me, as if I didn't have a clue what it was like for her, which I probably didn't. After an awkward bit of silence, she said, 'When my mum comes in I'm going to tell her I don't want any more physio. Mum says I don't have to do it, if I don't want to. She says it can't be doing me any good, if it's hurting like that.'

Then, like an absolute *idiot*, I said, 'I don't think I agree with your mum.' See what I mean? I just couldn't let it go.

'I don't remember asking for *your* opinion!' Delia snapped.

Later that evening when she didn't come in to watch *Corrie*, I knew I'd definitely messed things up; and the next morning when she didn't call in before school to say hi. I really missed her and all that next day I just kept thinking, why am I so stupid? Why had I said all that stuff? It's not as if I don't know how irritating I can be. When Jo came in to do my pressure checks, I told her, 'I think I might have upset Delia.'

'That would not be too difficult,' Jo said.

I asked her what exactly was wrong with Delia, and why she wasn't getting better, but Jo told me she couldn't talk to me about another patient's treatment.

'If Delia's upset it won't be because of you, though,' she assured me.

'I think it might,' I insisted. 'Grandpa's always telling me, I never know when to let things go. It's a terrible tendency I have.'

Jo laughed and told me I was too hard on myself. 'You needn't worry, Chloe, Delia will soon come round.'

After she'd gone I was still feeling bad and I kept wishing I could have that conversation with Delia back again and do it differently. I spent the rest of the afternoon practising what I would say, if I did get another chance. I was watching the clock, waiting for three o'clock, but it came and went and there was still no sign of Delia.

Daniel came in for an hour between four and five and we did some maths, but my heart wasn't in it.

When Delia did turn up around teatime Daniel went off and left us to it, but I didn't get chance to apologise, because she'd brought someone with her – a boy called Robbie.

I was really disappointed; I didn't want this boy there. I wanted Delia on her own so that I could make sure things were OK between us. But actually she didn't look cross with me; it was as if she'd already forgotten we'd fallen out.

I wondered how Delia and Robbie had got to know each other so quickly, because they were talking and laughing as if they were old friends. Then I found out that they were – he'd been on Ward 14 before too.

I tried not to stare at Robbie, but it was difficult because he was covered in scars, on his face and his hands and arms. Quite a lot of his skin was red and a bit raw-looking. He wore a baseball cap pulled down right over his face, but apart from that he didn't seem too bothered about how he looked. He was grinning a lot and making Delia laugh.

'Robbie had an accident with fireworks – *fifty per cent burns*,' Delia announced, almost proudly. 'He was lucky to get off alive. He had loads of skin grafts. He's in to have them fiddled with.'

'It's called scar revision,' Robbie added.

'Whatever! Chloe just got knocked down by a bus,' Delia told Robbie, as if mine was only a two-star accident compared to his five-star disaster. I didn't bother correcting Delia, it wasn't the bus that hit me.

She tried to get Robbie to tell me all the details of his accident, but he brushed that aside and said, 'No, I want to hear how come *she* gets out of lessons. I'd like a bit of that.'

'It's because I'm home-schooled,' I told him.

'Is that 'cos of your accident?'

'No, it has nothing to do with that,' I explained. 'I've pretty well always been taught at home, by my parents.'

Robbie asked why, so I said, 'Because...it just works better for all of us.'

'So what do you do all day? Skive? I know I would.'

That really annoyed me. 'I do lessons,' I said, 'the same as you, only I do them on my own.'

'Boring,' he said.

'But I can do whatever I feel like doing,' I said, 'not what someone else decides I ought to be doing because it's eleven o'clock on a Thursday morning.'

'Still sounds boring to me,' Robbie said, grinning.

'If you've got to do lessons anyway, what's the point? May as well go to school. School's better.'

I felt really irritated then. How could he know it was better? I wished Delia hadn't invited him into my room. He was getting me so mad.

'I don't know what you're basing that on,' I said.

'You said, yourself, you're on your own all day. That can't be any fun.'

'Well, it suits me,' I told him. 'I don't get distracted by other people and I don't waste time on things that I don't have any interest in. I can work until nine o'clock at night if I feel like it, or I can spend the whole day reading. It's up to me. How can school be better than that?'

Delia said, 'She's got you there, Robbie. I wouldn't argue with Chloe, if I were you, she has an answer for everything. She's a regular brain-box.'

But that just seemed to make Robbie more determined than ever. He tried to make school sound like your birthday and Christmas rolled into one. I know I'd only tried it for a while but I knew that wasn't a true picture and I told him so.

Robbie grinned, as if I'd caught him out, but he still wouldn't drop the subject. He started asking me the most stupid questions you ever heard: Did I have to call my mum Miss? Did I have to ask if I wanted to go to the toilet? Did she call a register? Did I wear a uniform? Was I allowed to eat in class? Did I get detentions and have to write lines? Could I just go to the fridge and help myself whenever I felt like it? Honestly!

'One of the best things about being home-schooled,' I told him, 'is that there *are* no petty rules and stupid traditions. Nobody has to make me work, because I want to learn anyway.' And I kept on like that until I realised what a stupid goody-goody I was starting to sound like.

Robbie stood there grinning, as if I was making half of it up, which got me so mad that we ended up almost shouting at each other and in the middle of it all, Marian walked in.

She stood there looking so odd and awkward and all I could think was that I wished she'd washed her hair and wasn't wearing that old mac.

I couldn't help wondering what Delia and Robbie were thinking of her. I was about to introduce them, but Robbie butted in. 'Hi,' he said. 'You must be Chloe's mum. I'd take off my cap, but believe me you'd wish I hadn't, unless you've got a strong stomach, that is.'

When he saw Marian's horrified face Robbie quickly apologised. 'Sorry, I forget not everyone gets my sense of humour. It's a bit black, I suppose.'

Marian still didn't seem to know what to say so Robbie added, 'Come on, Dee, we'd better get back on the ward, before Jo comes looking for us. See you later, Einstein,' he grinned at me. 'You must be a pretty good teacher,' he told Marian. 'You've done a good job on her.'

Even Marian smiled at that, but after they'd gone she said, 'I never know who I'm going to find when I come in here these days, Chloe.' I could see that she was trying to make a joke of it, but she didn't look as if she thought it was funny. I just smiled and shrugged. 'I'm not really sure that having all these children in and out of your room is such a good idea, though,' she went on, 'not when you're trying to get better.'

'Oh, Marian,' I said, irritably. 'There are only two of them.'

'Well, you know how I worry about you...getting upset.'

I wanted to shout, *Well, don't worry about me – I'm not made of glass*, but, of course, I didn't, mainly because her eyes were doing that fast blinking thing that Daniel and I recognise as a bit of a danger sign – when she's starting to get stressed. I could see that now was probably not the best time to try again to get to the bottom of the *secrets* business. Instead I said, 'Marian, are you not sleeping again?' but she brushed that away.

'Is it because of Grandpa? ' I went on. 'Are you still worried about him?'

'He's getting worse,' she sighed. 'There's something going on. Has he told you anything?'

'No,' I said. 'Why would he?'

'Because he usually does.'

'*Did*,' I reminded her. 'Not any more.' I didn't think I'd better tell Marian how moody he'd been the day before. 'Anyway,' I said, 'you can at least stop worrying about me. I'm fine.'

I wasn't sure if she believed me, but her shoulders dropped a little and she let out her breath. 'I suppose so, but I'll be a lot happier when I get you home.'

'It's not so bad, now that I'm making friends,' I said, but Marian ignored that and changed the subject. After a couple of hours I did manage to persuade her that she could go home a bit earlier and I'd be fine.

'And promise me you won't go back into your lab,' I said. 'That you'll get an early night.'

'Yes, *Mum*,' she said grinning, and giving me a hug. 'But only if you'll do the same.'

I said I would; it's not like in hospital I had a lot of choice.

After Marian had gone I felt a bit guilty. I hadn't persuaded her to go home early just because I thought it would be good for her, but because I was hoping that Delia might come back to watch TV later.

And, even though we'd got off to a bit of a bad start, I was hoping she'd bring Robbie with her. I thought maybe – if I could just manage not to be irritating for five minutes and start arguing with him again – I might soon have not one friend, but two!

Chapter Twelve

To Infinity and Beyond

A PRIME NUMBER is one that has no factors – no numbers that exactly divide into it – except 1 and itself.

2...3...5...7...11...13...17...19...are all primes.

We know there are an infinite number of primes because centuries ago a famous mathematician called Euclid proved it.

Prime numbers sometimes occur together in a cluster: 101...103...107...109.

But between 90 and 100 there's only one: 97 and none between 199 and 211.

No matter how hard mathematicians have looked at prime numbers they have never been able to find a pattern – so far.

With so much time in hospital and not much to do but lie there thinking about things, I'd started getting a bit obsessed with secrets. I seemed to be seeing them everywhere – even in numbers.

I imagined that there might even be a pattern locked inside *prime numbers*, like a little secret, that no one had yet discovered. I mean, just suppose that you could follow them almost to infinity – you might find a pattern starts to emerge. It is possible.

Of course I know that there's no such point as *almost infinity* – it's a bit like an oxymoron, isn't it? That's the whole point of infinity: there is no *point* to go to! Sometimes at home I liked to just lie and dream about what infinity really means: the idea that numbers go on and on, forever and ever and ever and...ever!

Daniel says that even if you lined up all the computers in the world – end to end – and ran the biggest and fastest programmes you could devise, they could never reach the end of counting numbers. Even if you ran them till the computers died of old age they still wouldn't have made the slightest impression on exhausting infinity. That kind of thing makes my brain tingle.

One of the great things about being home-schooled is that I'm allowed to do things like that and nobody thinks I'm wasting time. Daniel or Marian may ask me what I'm doing, but if I say, 'Dreaming about infinity,' they won't say, 'Well, do something useful instead.'

It's about respect, Marian says: respecting the fact that *I* know what's good for *me*, deciding for myself how I can best spend my time – and no one interfering in that.

Because the five of us live so closely together – well, the four of us now that Grandma's died – Marian has always said that it's important we respect each other's opinions, even when we don't agree with them, and each other's privacy, which is why we each have our own bits of space.

I have my two domains: my bedroom and The Log, where I can go and be exactly how I want to be. No one comes into those spaces unless I want them to.

Daniel's study is sort of his sacred space. I'm allowed to go in there, if I want to, but I know that Daniel likes me to knock first to give him time to turn his mathematician's brain off and be ready to talk about ordinary things like – has he remembered that it's Thursday, which is his day to make supper, because it's gone six-thirty and Marian and I are getting hungry?

I go in and out of Marian's lab all the time, but in the same way I try to decide whether it's a good time to disturb her. If she looks really involved in what she's doing, I may come back later. But if I really need her, she'll always stop what she's doing. Marian says there is nothing so important it can't wait for a hug.

Right from when I was little I was always encouraged to check out with Grandma and Grandpa if it was OK to visit them, before going in. They always used to say yes, anyway, because they seemed to like having me chattering away while they got on with jobs and things, but I always knocked first, just in case.

It's not because anyone has anything to hide, Marian said – like secrets and things – and I'd always believed that until recently.

Now I'd started to go back over all sorts of things that had happened before my accident, trying to find clues. You know, the kinds of things that didn't ever quite add up at the time, that you couldn't make sense of?

There was one day, after Grandma had died, but before things got difficult between Grandpa and me, when he was very odd with me and wouldn't let me see one of his orchids. At the time I had no idea what that was about, but it began to fit into this sort of theory I was building.

We were in one of the hothouses. Grandpa had

been telling me again the story of how he started off with just one plant on his kitchen windowsill twenty years ago, before the orchid bug bit him, and how these days he and Marian have four enormous glasshouses with thousands and thousands of plants.

I'd probably been wittering on as usual, plaguing Grandpa with questions, because he suddenly pointed to a new hybrid he was expecting to come into flower any day and said, 'I think I'll call this one *Chloe's Never-ending Questions.*'

'Marian says that's how you learn,' I told him, grinning.

'It's how you drive other people to distraction,' Grandpa grumbled. 'You know your problem? You're just like these orchids.'

'How?' I said, surprised.

'Artificially raised under unnatural conditions.'

I've always known Grandpa thinks it's a weird way for me to grow up – not going to school and without friends – but I thought he was just making a bit of a joke, as usual, so I said, 'Oh, well, if it's good enough for the orchids...'

But he really turned on me. 'That's different, for goodness' sake. These are just plants, they're not important, but you are. You should have had a normal life – if things had been different – if your mother wasn't...'

He sort of trailed off when he realised how angry he sounded, and reached out and ruffled my hair. 'Oh, it's not your fault. You can't help being born into a mad family. Come on, flower,' he said, 'I'll write some labels and you put them in the pots.'

For once I managed not to plague Grandpa with more questions. But a little later, when I was standing on the stepladders making space for the new plants on a high shelf, I came across an orchid I was sure I'd never seen before. I don't think Grandpa realised that it had come into flower because it was still tucked away, out of sight, which was a shame because it was so beautiful.

'This is one I don't recognise,' I said, reaching up to turn the label towards me, but before I had chance to read it, Grandpa came over and almost lifted me down.

'Never mind that,' he said. 'Leave it alone.'

'It's so pretty,' I said. 'What's it called?'

'Infernal questions all the time,' he snapped. 'I told you to leave it alone.'

Grandpa pushed the orchid right to the back of the shelf where I definitely couldn't reach it.

'I don't understand what the big secret is,' I smiled, trying to make a joke of it, and asked, 'Can I think of a name for it?'

Grandpa looked like I'd caught him out. 'It's already got a name,' he mumbled, and suddenly there were tears in his eyes.

I didn't ask him any more, but the next time I went in there, I have to admit, I did go looking for it. Well, I can't help being curious. I climbed up on the stepladders and searched all along the back of the shelf, but it had gone.

When I described to Marian how odd Grandpa had been, she gave me an odd look, too. She pretended she was busy and peered down her microscope, but I could see there was nothing on the slide.

'It was probably one of his illegal ones,' she said after a while.

'They're not *really* illegal, are they?' I said.

Lots of people like Grandpa own orchids that they've had since long before these new rules came in, that they haven't always got the paperwork for, even though they bought them perfectly legally in the first place. But now those plants are suddenly considered illegal and if anyone tried to move them outside the country they could be arrested! 'It's not like they're still taking orchids from the wild,' I said. 'These are old plants. It's so stupid.'

'Even stupid laws are still the law,' Marian said.

But somehow I knew this wasn't one of *those* orchids. Grandpa doesn't hide those from me, because he knows I'm on his side. There was something else about this one, some other reason why it was such a big secret. I began to think it was connected to Grandpa and Marian's secret and that made me more and more determined to get to the bottom of it.

Even before Grandma died we'd all spent bits of time on our own, in our own separate domains, but over a year after she'd died, it felt as if we were living most of the time in our own separate worlds – like little satellites revolving round each other. At odd times we might coincide, and things might be the way they used to, but a bit like *prime numbers*, it felt random, as if there wasn't any kind of pattern.

Being home-schooled had always meant that each day was different from the one before, and that was good. My days had never been timetabled, or predictable in that way, but there was more of a pattern to them and I missed that. Now each day had begun to feel like the one before – weeks drifting into one other, not so much leading on to infinity as going round and round in a never-ending loop.

Grandma dying had changed things, but it was more than that. I know that Daniel always tells me you shouldn't rely just on feelings, but something didn't *feel* right and I couldn't work out what it was.

I suppose that was why I'd started to think that maybe, just possibly, I'd give school another try. Now that I was older maybe I'd settle better. I decided not to mention anything to Marian and Daniel, not until I'd made up my mind. It felt strange having a proper secret from them, but for now that was the way I wanted to keep it – to myself.

Chapter Thirteen

The way Delia was glaring into her bowl of cereal you'd have thought the nurses were out to poison her. Now that we were friends again, she was bringing her breakfast into my room before school each morning. Delia was never very happy when it came round to nine o'clock, but this particular morning she really didn't want to go.

I wasn't in the best of moods either, because I'd had an argument with Marian the night before. When she asked me what I'd been up to, I'd said, 'Hanging out with Delia and Robbie.'

She nearly jumped down my throat. 'I can guess where you got that silly expression from. And why you've suddenly started talking in that ridiculous fashion.'

I knew what Marian meant, although I hadn't

realised I was doing it. One of the first things I'd asked Robbie was why all his sentences went up at the end like questions, even when they weren't.

'Where have you been living?' he asked. 'Don't you ever watch TV?'

'It's like in Australian soaps,' Delia explained. 'Loads of people at my school do it as well.'

'*Everyone*,' said Robbie.

'But why would you want to be the same as everyone else?' I asked.

'To fit in, *obviously*,' Robbie said, 'otherwise you get picked on, or left out, or treated like you're a dork.'

'If you went to my school you'd better fit in or else,' Delia agreed.

And I suppose that's what I'd started doing, without realising it – trying to fit in with Robbie and Delia. Marian didn't like it at all.

'I'm not happy about the way you seem to be changing,' she said.

'The way I talk you mean?'

'Not just that.'

'Don't you *ever* want me to have friends?' I asked.

'Oh, don't be silly. It's not that at all,' Marian insisted.

'But you've never encouraged me to,' I told her. 'Not like Grandma and Grandpa did.'

'Yes, well, we know how their attempts backfired – *and* all the other times. Look, sweetheart, I hate to see you getting hurt. I'm only thinking of you.'

I knew Marian meant it; her eyes were full of tears, but I just turned away. And when she went home I'd still not really forgiven her.

Until now, I'd always believed that it was my fault that I couldn't make friends – probably because I was too weird, or *different*, Marian would have said. But since I'd met Delia and Robbie I couldn't see any real reason why I shouldn't make friends. So maybe Marian and Daniel had their own reasons for not wanting me to. And maybe those reasons were connected to the secret too.

It was all really beginning to bug me – which was another expression I'd learned from Delia – especially whenever I was with my family. Delia, even in her current bad temper, was far easier to be around. I tried cheering her up with my famous chicken impression, but I could hardly raise a smile.

'It's not fair,' she grumbled, pushing aside her cereal. 'I don't see why Robbie gets to stay and hang out in your room all day while I have to go and sit in boring old lessons.'

'You know why,' I said, smiling. It was because Robbie's school had sent work in for him to be getting on with. His operation for scar revision had been postponed for a couple of days because he'd developed a skin infection and they had to wait for that to clear up, but he didn't seem to mind. 'I thought you said it was OK, better than your regular school, anyway.'

'Which only makes it a bit less boring,' she snapped. Then she said something that surprised me: 'I was your friend first – before *Robbie*.'

'Well, it was you that introduced us,' I reminded her, laughing, which clearly wasn't the right thing to say, because she scowled at me.

'Yeah, well, *now* I wish I hadn't!'

I began to wonder how other kids managed more than one friend at a time. It was really difficult.

'You're still my best friend,' I told her, which cheered her up, until Robbie came bouncing in with his files and notepad and Delia's face clouded over again.

'Are you going to show me another of those maths tricks?' Robbie asked.

'OK,' I said, but when Delia narrowed her eyes at me and tightened her lips I added, 'or we could wait till Delia gets back from school.' That seemed to be the right thing to say, although I wasn't sure why. Delia had never shown any interest in maths games before.

Robbie shrugged. 'Whatever,' he said.

'I'll see you two later, then,' Delia said. 'Just make sure you don't talk about anything without me.'

'About *anything*?' Robbie said. 'That's a tall order.'

'You know what I mean,' she snapped.

As Delia left, Robbie rolled his eyes and grinned at me. I didn't grin back – that would have felt disloyal. Instead I asked Robbie how he felt about having his surgery postponed for a couple more days.

'Suits me,' he said, 'I don't care how many times they put it off.'

'Is that because it's going to be painful?' I asked.

Robbie laughed, 'Of course it's going to hurt a bit, but *that* doesn't bother me.'

'It would bother me,' I admitted. 'I wouldn't want to swop with you.'

'Nor me,' Robbie agreed. 'That'd be way too scary.'

I asked him what he meant by that.

'There's no way I could survive without mates!' he

explained. 'It'd be like living on a desert island. I'm not saying that's what it's like for you. Everybody's different, right? But that would scare me more than a dozen operations.'

'My life's not that bad,' I said, trying to defend myself. 'I've got other things...'

'Yeah, I know...maths,' Robbie said, rolling his eyes. 'Not quite the same, Chloe.'

I didn't push it, instead I said, 'Even so, I still would have thought you'd want to get it over with.'

But he said, 'It's not going to be over with, though, is it? I'll have to have these scar revisions all the time I'm growing up. And, even then, it's not like I'm ever going to look normal again, so what's the point? I'll always look pretty gross!'

I didn't think he looked gross and I told him so. 'I was a bit shocked the first time I met you,' I admitted, 'but already I hardly notice. I think you've got a nice face.'

Robbie grinned, 'I hope you're not coming on to me?'

I think he could tell from my blank face I didn't know what that meant.

'It's what you call a joke, OK? Honest, Chloe, sometimes it feels like explaining the world to an alien. Anyway, I'm getting used to how I look, I'm not that bothered. I'm just fed up about missing footie and this weekend I'm missing the trials for a new team. I don't *want* to have it done right now.'

'Well, why do you have to?'

'To keep everyone else happy, of course; so my family don't have to feel guilty.'

At the risk of seeming like an alien again, I asked, 'Why would *they* feel guilty?'

Robbie explained that the fireworks had come from his mum and dad's shop and his kid brother had been the one fooling around with them, who'd caused the accident in the first place. So I could understand his problem.

'You'll just have to put a brave face on it then,' I joked, without realising quite what I'd said. 'Oh, Robbie, I'm sorry, I didn't really mean that...' but I still couldn't help grinning. Fortunately nor could he.

'Forget it,' he said. 'I'll get my own back later.'

I suppose, because Robbie had told me so much about himself, I started to tell him what was most on my mind.

First of all I had to admit that all those things I'd said – about how brilliant being home-schooled was – didn't give the full picture.

'I guessed that,' Robbie said, grinning.

'So I've been wondering lately whether maybe you were right,' I said, 'and I ought to give school another chance.'

Then Robbie admitted that he might have exaggerated too. 'School sure isn't a bed of roses,' he said, 'but it has some things going for it, like friends, for instance, so I'd try it if I were you.'

'The trouble is: Marian and Daniel have always said that it's my choice, but I've got this feeling they don't really want me to go. I used to think it was just because Marian's so overprotective of me, but now I think there's something else going on.'

'Like what?'

'I don't know.'

'Well, like you said, it's your choice, so you're going to have to *put your foot down* and *stand on your own two feet!*'

'Oh, very amusing,' I said, throwing my hat at him – my stripey woollen one with a long tail and a monkey climbing up it. Robbie put it on and threw me his baseball cap. We spent the rest of the day wearing each other's hats, mostly getting on with our work, but chatting some of the time. It was really nice – just *be-ing* with someone else.

When Delia came back from school she couldn't see the joke. She said, 'Do you have any idea what idiots you both look?'

Robbie just grinned at her, and swung the bobble around in a cheeky way, but Delia still didn't smile.

'We can do one of those maths tricks,' Robbie said, 'now that her ladyship's back.' But after all the fuss she'd made earlier, Delia didn't look that interested to be honest.

I've probably told you how I have this irritating habit of bumbling on sometimes. I started off by explaining all about this Italian mathematician who devised a series of numbers named after him: the Fibonacci series, in which each number is the sum of the two preceding digits, for example: 1, 1, 2, 3, 5, 8, 13, 21...but Robbie said, 'Cut to the chase, Chloe. You're telling us more than we want to know.'

So I just grinned and got on with the puzzle.

I told them to write down any two numbers one above the other, for example 4 and 9, and add them to make a third number (13), then add the second and third to make a fourth number ($9+13=22$) and to keep doing that until they had ten numbers written in a column and then to draw a line underneath. I told them not to let me see the paper until they'd finished. When they handed it to me, within two seconds I was able to tell them the sum of all ten figures.

Robbie was impressed, Delia just looked confused. Things had started to get difficult when Robbie told Delia she was being dim. I tried to keep the peace, like Daniel often does. When Robbie had wanted to do it all in his head, I'd told him it had to be on paper, because I somehow knew that Delia would struggle to calculate in her head. As it was, she still complained that she couldn't keep up, because we were going too fast.

Robbie had started with 6 and 9. I just took a glance at his column of figures and told him the answer: 1,122. Delia had chosen 5 and 7 and I told her that hers was 891.

It took them far longer to check that I was right, especially Delia, but in the end they agreed that I was. Every time we tried a new set of figures I got it right.

'OK, there's got to be a trick to it,' Robbie insisted.

'Of course there's a trick,' I said and explained that

all you had to do was look at the fourth figure from the bottom in the column and multiply it by 11.

I admitted that I didn't exactly know why it worked, but it does, every time. It's the beauty of the Fibonacci series. 'But one day I will understand why it works,' I said.

'That's pretty cool,' Robbie told me.

I knew that was quite a compliment coming from Robbie, but Delia sort of spoiled it by bursting out laughing.

'I'm not being horrible, or anything,' she said, 'but I don't think you could call Chloe *cool* exactly. She's really nice, but there's no way she's *cool*.'

'I don't know,' said Robbie, 'I think Chloe's so un-cool, it's quite cool.'

I don't think I understood that, nor did Delia, but she didn't have time to argue because just then her pain specialist nurse came looking for her.

'I might have guessed where I'd find you,' Katie said, smiling. 'It's time for your physio.'

'I've only just got out of school. Can't I do it later? Please?' Delia begged.

'Come on, Dee, you know you need to keep up with these exercises.'

'But I hate them. Mum says I don't have to do them, if I don't want to.' She was almost in tears. 'It's not fair.'

But Katie wouldn't take no for an answer. 'Come on, the sooner you get them done, the sooner you can be back with your friends,' she said, wheeling Delia away.

A little while later Delia's mum put her head round the door, looking for her. Robbie told her that Delia had gone along for her physio. Her mum rolled her eyes. 'I don't know why they keep putting her through all this extra pain when it isn't doing her any good. I've a good mind to take her home. It would certainly save me a lot of hassle,' she went off grumbling.

'Poor old Delia,' I said to Robbie. 'She must be so sick of hospitals.'

'Tell me about it,' said Robbie.

'At least you get to go home between operations. She's been in here nearly three months! I don't understand why she isn't getting better. I wish we could help her.'

'Yeah, sure,' Robbie agreed, 'but how?'

'I don't know, but there must be a way. Every problem has a solution,' I told him. 'It's just about finding the right strategy.'

But Robbie didn't agree. 'All problems don't have a solution,' he said. 'Some things can't be put right and sometimes you have to learn to live with them.'

'That sounds like giving up to me,' I said.

'Not necessarily, it's about getting on with your life. Before the accident I had friends, sure, but I was sort of Mr Average. Now everyone in my school knows who I am. People notice me. I feel more...me. So that's a good thing.'

'Well, it doesn't seem to be working like that for Delia,' I said. 'She hates being here.'

'Well, she says that, but maybe if you had seven brothers and sisters like her you wouldn't be in such a hurry to go home,' Robbie said.

'She never told me she had seven brothers and sisters!' I said, amazed. I couldn't imagine what that might be like.

'Well, maybe it's not that. Maybe there's some other reason, some other mystery. Most families have them.'

It really threw me when Robbie said that, it felt as if he'd been able to read my mind. I hadn't planned on telling him, but I found myself doing it.

'I think there's some mystery in *my* family,' I said, and I told him the things I'd overheard that first night in hospital and the little bits I'd started to piece together: Grandpa being so secretive over his orchid, and Grandma calling me Libby, and about the time Grandpa told me that there were lots of things I didn't know. They seemed such small, insignificant clues taken separately, but put together they might mean something.

'I know it's not much to go on,' I said, 'but I've just got this *feeling* they're connected.'

'Always trust your gut feelings,' Robbie told me. 'I do.'

'That's not what Daniel says. He says you should never rely on feelings alone, you should always look for evidence.'

'Well, you haven't got very much of that, so far,' Robbie said. 'So if I were you, I wouldn't waste my time playing at Miss Marple, I'd just ask straight out.'

I sighed; it sounded so easy. But I hadn't managed it so far. I couldn't explain to Robbie how difficult it felt to risk upsetting Marian, especially the state she was in at the moment.

Earlier that day I'd finished reading *Jane Eyre* and I couldn't stop thinking about Mr Rochester's mad wife.

I'm not saying Marian was anything like *her*. But ever since I was little, I'd known how important it was not to do anything that might upset Marian. All the family seemed to know that.

Since Grandma died, though, it didn't seem to matter how much I tried not to worry her, Marian still got tense and upset, and since my accident more than ever. And now, being away from Marian, I could see it so much more clearly.

I couldn't tell Robbie, or Delia, any of that, of course. I didn't want to risk losing my first real friends, which was probably what would happen, once they found out what a very weird family I came from.

Chapter Fourteen

You Don't Have to be Mad, But it Helps!

For a long time there were only whole numbers and fractions of whole numbers.

These were called RATIONAL NUMBERS.

Eventually mathematicians had to accept the idea that there might be something which was neither a whole number nor a fraction.

These were called IRRATIONAL NUMBERS.

The most famous example is the number π (which is written pi and pronounced pie), which relates the diameter of a circle (d) to its circumference (c): $c = \pi \times d$

π is worth a little bit more than 3 - approximately 3.14 — but it can't ever be given an exact value because the number of decimal places it can be calculated to goes on to infinity:

3.1415926535897932384626433832705028841971693993

and still counting...

Can you believe that mathematicians have calculated π to over eight billion places already, and some are still working on it?

'That could drive a person crazy!' I tell Daniel.

'Well, you don't have to be mad to be a mathematician,' he jokes, 'but it certainly helps.'

According to some of Daniel's stories there have been quite a few mathematicians throughout history that were more than a bit crazy.

Pythagoras, the famous Greek mathematician, refused to accept *irrational numbers* – he considered them far too weird. He even allowed one of his students to be put to death when he kept trying to convince everyone they really existed.

Archimedes, another brilliant mathematician, became more and more obsessed as he grew older. According to the legend, when the Roman army invaded the town where he lived, and soldiers forced their way into his home, Archimedes was so wrapped up in his maths that he hardly noticed, and when he failed to answer the soldiers' questions he was speared to death.

Even I'm not so crazy about maths I'd let myself be speared to death!

Grandpa's orchid stories, just like Daniel's, are full of crazy characters who risked their lives to chase rare and exotic plants half way across the world.

Perhaps, to be the very best at something, you have to be completely obsessed, or a little bit mad, or both. A genius is probably never going to be an ordinary sort of person, living an ordinary sort of life. Marian and Daniel often tell me that it usually involves some kind of effort or sacrifice to achieve anything really worthwhile—but that it's always worth it.

On his study door, Daniel has a poster that says:

'A problem worthy of attack

Proves its worth by fighting back'

To be a perfectionist, Daniel says, you have to love the challenge, but most of all you have to enjoy the process.

One day in hospital, when I was feeling a bit dozy and not up to much, Jo came in and asked me if I wanted her to put the TV on for me, but I said, 'No, thanks. I'm not that bothered.'

'So if you're not into TV, what do you like, Chloe?' she asked.

I'm sure it's just going to make me sound even weirder, but I told her that what I love best is to get completely lost in something – a calculation, or a really good story, or some fascinating facts I've been learning. You know, when you suddenly find that the room has gone dark and you haven't realised that hours have gone by and you've been completely absorbed inside your own head? I love that feeling.

Jo smiled at me, with her head on one side and said, 'You are an odd one, Chloe, and that's a fact.' She was smiling, but I couldn't tell whether she was saying that *odd* was OK, or not. I think odd is OK; I'm not so sure about weird; I know *weirdo* definitely isn't.

When I walk home from the village, I have to walk along the edge of an estate. There's a small park, where some kids my age sometimes hang out. They don't bully me exactly, but they often shout things like: *it's that weirdo*. I try not to take any notice, like Marian tells me, but it's difficult.

I know that I must be a bit weird, because I've been told it a few times now. So I looked up the word in dictionaries and a thesaurus, and it was very confusing. Sometimes it said things like – *remarkable and interesting*, which sounds good, doesn't it? Even *mysterious* could be, and I wasn't too worried by *strange*, *odd* and *eccentric*. But *misfit, crank, barmy, loony, oddball, freak* are horrible.

The one that worried me most though, is *mad*.

It says in *Jane Eyre* that Mr Rochester's wife's

madness ran in her mother's family through three generations. If I could choose, I'd probably rather take after my dad. Daniel often behaves like a funny, absent-minded professor, but doesn't actually seem *mad* at all, whereas Marian sometimes does. But I had this growing feeling that it's actually Marian that I take after and maybe that's why I'd always felt different to other kids and found it so difficult to get on with them – like Mary's granddaughter, Hayley.

Maybe that's what she meant when she said I wasn't quite right in the head, and what Grandpa meant when he said that I couldn't help being born into a mad family. Perhaps he was being serious.

I began to wonder – what if *that* was the big secret: that I'm a bit mad – like Marian – and they were all frightened to tell me? And what about Libby? Was she mad too? Is that the reason no one ever talked about her?

Irrational is another word that people sometimes use when they're talking about mad behaviour, which is quite different to what we mean when we talk about *irrational numbers* in maths.

In the dictionary it says that the meaning of irrational is *not endowed with reason – illogical – absurd.*

Well, I'm good at logic, and excellent at reasoning things out, Daniel says, and I don't feel *absurd*. Although I've never *felt* mad before, either. But now I was starting to wonder: would a person *know* they were mad – if they actually were?

Chapter Fifteen

Being in hospital was starting to feel like being in a parallel universe, as if outside my room, and beyond my bed, nothing else existed. I'd been stuck in it for nearly a month! It was difficult to imagine the world, well, my bit of world, still going on out there, without me.

Whenever my leg was hurting, or I was feeling homesick, or scared, I'd try to picture The Log and imagine myself back there in the garden, but I was starting to forget what it was like.

I could hardly guess what the weather outside was, because my window looked onto other hospital buildings and I couldn't even see the sky. I was starting to lose track of how long I'd been in there. So when Marian said, 'You haven't forgotten it's your birthday on Wednesday, have you?' in fact, I had.

Marian had already talked to Jo about bringing in a birthday cake for me, and then Jo had mentioned it in front of Robbie, and the next thing I knew, he and Delia had decided to organise a party for me!

I think the nurses liked the fact that the three of us had made friends; Jo said it kept us all occupied which made less work for them – until we started asking for things like parties, of course!

Robbie, who seemed to be able to get anything he wanted out of the nurses, managed to persuade them to let him and Delia organise a bit of party food in the nurses' kitchen: popcorn and crisps and fizzy drinks – things I wasn't usually allowed to have.

The very best thing of all was that they also agreed to let us have a sleepover, well, Delia and me anyway. I didn't really know what it meant when Delia first suggested it.

'How can you not know about sleepovers?' she demanded. 'It's where you sleep at a friend's house, and have a midnight feast and stay awake for like *hours* and talk in the dark,' which didn't sound so exciting to me, but Delia said, 'It's exciting, believe me. It's the best.'

The nurses said they'd put an extra bed in my room and Trish, who was on night duty and has a real soft spot for Robbie, said he could stay up late with us, as long as we didn't get up to any mischief, or disturb the other kids.

'Now, would we?' Robbie asked clasping his hands together, looking like a cross between an angel and a choirboy.

We wanted to start early, around seven o'clock, to give us more time but that was the time that everyone's family usually visited. Robbie and Delia said, no problem, they'd sort it with their parents so it was a bit embarrassing when Marian was the only one who made a fuss.

'But we *always* spend birthdays together. It's our special family time,' she reminded me, making me feel really guilty. But Daniel persuaded Marian that if they came in a little earlier we could still have plenty of family time.

I was relieved that when they did come in the next night, armed with presents and a cake and things, Marian was all smiles – until she spotted the spare bed under the window.

'What's that doing in here?'

'Delia's going to have a sleepover with me tonight,' I told her. 'The nurses said it would be OK.'

'Nobody asked us,' Marian said, looking anxious again. 'I don't think it's a good idea.'

'Why not?' I asked.

'You've had a serious accident is why not. Anyway, I can't see the point.'

'For goodness' sake, Marian,' Grandpa groaned.

'I'd just like to know what they're going to be getting up to,' Marian said, trying to sound more reasonable.

'What can we possibly get up to,' I asked her, 'with me in traction?!'

'Give the girl a break,' Grandpa said, and soon he and Marian were bickering again.

'Just leave this to us, Dad, it isn't up to you.'

'More's the pity,' Grandpa muttered. 'If it was she'd have had a bit more of this kind of normality in her life.'

'Come on, Marian. It's Chloe's birthday,' Daniel reminded her. 'She's twelve years old, she just wants to have some fun. I seem to remember you used to enjoy a party.'

'She was a tearaway,' Grandpa agreed. 'I remember her twenty-first when she jumped in the river with all her clothes on. We thought she'd catch her death of cold.'

Marian tried to stay serious, but in the end, she couldn't help smiling at the memory. 'I just hope the nurses keep a close eye on them, that's all.'

'I'm sure they will,' Daniel smiled.

'She'll have a great time,' Grandpa said, winking at me.

'I still wished we'd been asked about it,' Marian said.

Honestly, it's *my* birthday, I wanted to tell her, not yours. If Daniel and Grandpa could feel happy for me, why couldn't she? I wished Marian would just for once treat me as if I was a normal person – not breakable, like glass or too weird to be trusted around other kids.

This is how they'd always made me feel – that something terrible might happen if they didn't keep their eyes on me every minute. I couldn't ask now, not on my birthday, but if there was something bad about this secret, and it was to do with me, they had no right to keep it from me.

After I'd opened all my presents and we'd had a piece of cake, a part of me couldn't wait for them all to leave and I think Marian must have been able to tell, because she said, 'Well, I suppose we'd better go. I can see your friends hovering around outside.'

I could see them too, or at least Robbie leaning against the door waiting to come in.

When Marian came over to give me a hug, her eyes were suddenly full of tears. 'Happy birthday, sweetheart,' she said, and hugged me, as if she was never going to see me again. 'Have a lovely time. Don't make yourself sick, will you?'

'Honestly, Marian, it's only a few crisps and a bit of popcorn,' I said. 'I'm not going to die from a bit of junk food!'

That was obviously the wrong thing to say, because she had this terrible look on her face. Daniel squeezed Marian's shoulder. 'It was a joke, Marian,' he said. 'Come on, we're holding up the party. Have a lovely time,' he told me.

'I wish I was twelve again,' said Grandpa.

Delia and Robbie hardly waited for everyone to go before they piled in with plates and cups and presents and Delia's CD player! It was excellent.

Delia gave me a CD of greatest hits. 'You may be a brain-box,' she said, 'but you've got a lot of catching up to do in the cool music department.'

She put it straight on – really loud! In minutes the nurses were telling us to turn it down, which I was quite relieved about to be honest.

Robbie gave me a Terry Pratchett book. He'd already

told me he'd read every one he's written and when I said I'd never heard of him, Robbie almost choked. 'Clearly then, there's plenty you don't know, Einstein.'

'Party games are going to be a bit of a challenge,' Robbie announced, 'with Delia in a wheelchair and you confined to bed, but I've had a few ideas.'

They mostly involved us doing forfeits, like me balancing grapes on my nose and Delia drinking out of the wrong side of a glass and spilling it all down her and other silly things. I hadn't drunk fizzy drinks much before. I couldn't believe how quickly they filled me up with bubbles. Because I was half lying down it made me burp a lot and Robbie and Delia seemed to find that hilarious.

One of Delia's favourite songs came on and she bounced about in her wheelchair. 'It's not much of a party with no dancing is it?' she grumbled, looking down at her legs. 'I don't think I'll ever get to dance again.'

'Of course you will,' Robbie told her.

'What kind of dancing did you use to do?' I asked.

'*Dancing!*' Delia said, as if that would have been enough explanation for anybody but an alien. 'She doesn't even know about dancing! Show her, Robbie.'

'Me? I'm no dancer,' he told Delia. 'You show her.'

'Get real!" Delia snapped, as if he'd suggested she do a few acrobatics.

'You can show her the arms at least,' he coaxed her.

In the end Delia couldn't resist him. She sort of swayed from side to side and moved her arms to the music. It looked great.

'I couldn't do that,' I said, watching enviously.

'Well not at the moment, obviously,' said Robbie, trying to copy her.

'Don't worry,' Delia told me, smiling, 'as soon as you're back on your feet, I'll teach you. We'll have a proper sleepover at my house and we'll go dancing.'

I tried to picture a life where I went to stay at Delia's house – where she had seven brothers and sisters – and we went dancing. It felt like another universe entirely and to be honest I couldn't even imagine it. But it felt exciting.

'Now do the same sort of thing with your feet,' Delia told Robbie, 'but in time with your arms. Yeah, that's not bad, you could be a good mover,' she told him.

That made Robbie blush, so to cover it up he started wiggling his bottom, and making us giggle.

Trish and one of the other nurses peeped in, asked us to keep the noise down, then went away smiling.

Robbie soon got fed up with dancing on his own so he went over and pulled Delia to her feet. He told her to lean on him and he moved her around the room. Delia kept complaining but she looked as if she was loving it.

Watching them was the best fun I'd ever had!

Robbie was almost carrying Delia and he must have lost his balance because they nearly collided with the end of my bed. Robbie steadied himself in time, but a trolley next to my bed went crashing into the corner, which brought Trish running to see what was happening.

Robbie just grinned innocently over his shoulder at her. 'No damage,' he said, 'we just got a bit carried away.'

'*You* did,' Delia giggled.

'Just be careful, Robbie, that's all,' Trish smiled. 'Perhaps you'd better put her down now.'

'We're OK,' Delia said. 'It's good fun.'

'Well, that's fine, but there'll be no excuse tomorrow for not getting on those crutches,' Trish told Delia, smiling.

I don't think Delia liked that because as soon as

Trish had gone she made Robbie put her down and went very quiet.

'You haven't hurt yourself, have you?' I asked.

'No!' she snapped. 'But I hate those crutches. They needn't think I'm using them. They rub me.'

After that nothing Robbie could say or do would cheer her up.

'I'm tired; I'm going to bed,' she said, starting to move towards the door.

'What about the sleepover?' Robbie asked. 'You're not going to let Chloe down on her birthday, are you?'

Delia was fighting back tears. She said that her knee was killing her; that she just wanted to be on her own.

After she'd gone Robbie slumped in the chair by my bed. He looked up at the ceiling, but he didn't say anything and neither did I. Trish came in to see what had happened. She squeezed my hand and said, 'Looks like your sleepover's off, my darling.'

'I'd be up for it,' Robbie told Trish, grinning.

'Nice try, mister,' she told him, 'but it's time you were in bed.'

Robbie went off to get ready and Trish stayed to tidy up my room a bit.

'Well, did you enjoy that?' she asked.

'It was the best party I ever had,' I said. 'I feel bad about Delia, though.'

'Don't worry, she'll be fine in the morning; Delia usually bounces back. She's happy as long as no one puts any pressure on her, but that's not necessarily the way she's going to get better. Anyway, you've got a few nice cards,' she said, changing the subject.

'Ten!' I said. 'I can't believe it.' I'd had ones from Delia, Robbie, Gemma, Jo, even the night nurses had all signed one for me. I've kept all the birthday cards I've ever had in a box under my bed, but I'd never had more than five or six before, not on the same birthday.

It was a shame my party had ended like that – and the sleepover had been cancelled – but it was still the best birthday I'd ever had, certainly the noisiest – and the silliest.

It's strange, but my last birthday had ended badly too, with someone getting upset. I bet you can guess who that was.

Chapter Sixteen

In all Probability

Here's a party puzzle:
How many people do you think would need to
gather in the same room for it to be likely,
let's say an even chance, that two of them will
share the same birthday? What's your guess?
Since there are 365 days in a year, you might
guess 366. But that would be a certainty, not
a PROBABILITY.
In fact, the number needed to make it 50%
likely that the same birthday will occur twice,
is much smaller than you might imagine.
It's only 23. Can you believe that? I couldn't.

'The reason,' Daniel explained, 'is that although there are only 23 people in the room they can be organised into 253 different pairings, making the likelihood much greater. So you see, it isn't so surprising.'

It still surprised me. 'It goes completely against my intuition,' I complained.

Daniel smiled; intuition is something he's always telling me not to rely too heavily on. He's probably right – where maths is concerned anyway – but there are times when I wish I *had* trusted my intuition, like my birthday last year, for example.

Birthdays are always a big thing in my family, sort of sacred, really. It doesn't matter how busy the nursery is, or how involved Daniel is in his research, on birthdays everyone stops working and relaxes.

And if it's your birthday you get treated like a queen, or a king – you even get to wear the birthday crown, which gets covered with Grandpa's orchid flowers so that all through the party you're surrounded by the sweet smell of orchids.

You also get to choose the birthday theme. So, for example, when I was eight, and really into the Romans, everyone wrapped themselves in bed sheets, like togas, and we all lay on cushions and ate with our fingers. Grandma said she probably wouldn't choose to do it again – having to eat lying on the floor had given her terrible indigestion.

Another ritual we have is called *Hunting the Presents*. All your presents are hidden around the place and you're given cryptic clues, or coded messages, to help you find them. On Marian's last birthday, Daniel and I hid her presents so well she didn't find the last of them for two days, even though we kept giving her extra clues.

The other thing we do is to make *Birthday Wishes* which means writing down your hopes and ambitions, the things that you would like to do before your next birthday, then sealing them in an envelope and saving them for a year, then seeing how many you've managed to achieve.

That was the point last year when I wished I had listened to my intuition.

The theme had been *Blue*: my absolutely favourite colour at the time. Everything we wore, and ate, and drank, and even my presents had to be *blue*, which probably wasn't the best choice under the circumstances. I mean, blue's a bit of a cool colour, not exactly warm and jolly, and mine was the first birthday since Grandma had died two months before, so it was hard not to notice that she was missing. It all fell a little bit...flat.

Towards the end, Marian seemed to think it might liven things up if I opened my *Birthday Wishes* envelope from the year before, but I suddenly had this feeling it wasn't a good idea, even though I couldn't remember what I'd written on the list. I should have listened to myself.

Out of six things on the list, I'd only achieved two, which were both maths challenges. I hadn't managed any of the next three because Grandma had died: I hadn't passed my Grade Three piano exam, I hadn't got my 25-metre swimming badge and I'd never finished reading *Lord of the Rings*, which was one of the books she'd given me and now it made me too sad to read it without her.

As soon as I read them out everyone started thinking about Grandma and the fact that she wasn't there. Grandpa got very low and said, 'I'm feeling a bit tired, would you mind if I had an early night?'

By then, I have to say, the party atmosphere was quickly disappearing and we should have just given up on it, but Marian insisted I finish my list, as there was only one thing left on it.

I was quite surprised with the last item because I'd forgotten entirely that I'd even put it down. 'Number six,' I read out, 'decide about going to school.'

Then I remembered that it was the appalling Miss Morris who had put the idea in my head. A week before my last birthday she'd been on her annual visit to check up on me. She's a Special Adviser that the Education Authority sends to make sure Marian and Daniel are educating me properly. We all think she's a bit of an idiot to be honest. Marian's had a few arguments with her. She says that Miss Morris has no authority to interfere in what we're doing; she isn't even supposed to test my reading, but it doesn't stop her trying.

She's a bit creepy and she smells of cigarettes. I always try to sit as far away from her as I can. If Marian goes out of the room to make her a cup of tea, or answer the phone, she leans towards me and says things like, 'Well, Chloe, here's a little opportunity for you to show me what you and Mummy have been doing,' as if I'm about three and a half!

If I hesitate she says, 'Of course, you don't have to, if you don't want to; no pressure from me; your choice entirely.' And all the while she's saying it, she's picking up my books, and flicking through my projects, and looking round the room, and weaselling away like that until you think, oh, why not just show her and get it over with.

One time, when I was about seven, she wheedled

round me until I agreed to read to her, even though Marian said she didn't want me to. It must have been obvious – even to Miss Morris – that I was a good reader because of all the writing I'd done, but she seemed to think I couldn't be learning anything because Marian didn't believe in lesson plans and teaching me phonics and things. I don't know what got into me, but I went and got one of Daniel's Mathematical Bulletins, which I could just about read, even though I couldn't actually understand any of it. She soon got bored and told me to stop, but I kept on going for two whole pages. She's never asked me to read to her since then.

Miss Morris is always telling Marian that I should really be going to places where I might meet other children – youth clubs or the Guides.

'There's no point Chloe being hothoused in some areas,' she said, 'but deprived in others,' which absolutely made Marian's blood boil.

When I asked Marian what she'd meant by that, all she said was, 'The woman doesn't know what she's talking about. She wouldn't know a hothouse if she got locked in one, which she just might one of these days if she's not careful.'

Just before my tenth birthday, when Marian was out in the kitchen, Miss Morris asked me – yet again – if I wouldn't prefer to go to school and mix with other children, but this time she added, 'Because if you think it's something you might *ever* want to do, then next year is the obvious time – when other children will be changing schools and it would be much easier to integrate. Of course, it's your choice. I certainly wouldn't want to influence you, one way or the other. But you must realise that this isn't exactly an ideal situation, so I want you to promise you'll at least think about it.'

She whispered most of this because she knew that if Marian heard her she'd have chased her down the drive with a spray of weedkiller.

I didn't tell Marian, obviously; I didn't want to upset her. Anyway, I was quite happy as I was at that time. I only wrote it on my list because she'd made me promise that I would. And then it had gone out of my mind – until I read it out a year later and upset Marian so much.

'Daniel and I thought you were happy as you are.'

'I am,' I told her.

'I'd always thought you'd enjoyed our adventures, our voyages of discovery. We had such nice times, didn't we?' and her eyes filled up, remembering some of them.

'Yes,' I insisted, 'I did, I still do...'

'So why would you want to *spoil* everything?'

'*Change* everything,' Daniel corrected her, quietly.

'I don't know that I do. It's just that Miss Morris said...'

'Oh, I might have known she was behind this, interfering old busybody!'

'But I don't see what the problem is. You've always told me that it was my choice...' I tried again.

'And it is,' Daniel insisted.

'We thought you were happy with it,' Marian muttered, 'until now.'

'But we agreed to review it from time to time,' Daniel reminded Marian, patting her hand. 'So we should keep to that plan. But there's plenty of time,' he smiled at me. 'No point spoiling your party worrying about it now.'

I could see how bothered Marian was, but I was surprised that Daniel – who's always so careful about the words he uses – seemed to think it was something to worry about and that it would spoil my party to talk about it.

After that the party didn't ever really pick up – a Miss Morris-shaped cloud sort of hung over it.

Later that night, when I was lying in bed, I could hear Daniel and Marian's voices, low but clearly arguing, and Marian actually crying. I didn't know what I'd done to make her cry, but it must have had something to do with me going to school, which I found very confusing. Neither of them ever brought the subject up again, though, and I wasn't going to risk upsetting Marian by mentioning it either.

After that, I suppose I thought that *in all probability* I would carry on being home-schooled and be perfectly happy with that. I wasn't to know that I'd get knocked down by a four-by-four and end up in hospital, and make friends with Robbie and Delia, and find out about family secrets – in fact, have my whole world turned upside down.

It's like in maths problems: you think you know what the possible outcomes are, but then chance, or fate – or Jo would probably say God – takes over and everything changes and all you've got to rely on are your feelings – and your intuition. And if you can't trust that, then what do you do?

Chapter Seventeen

'Delia's disappeared,' Robbie announced, the morning after my birthday.

'Disappeared?'

'Run off home. Well, not exactly,' he grinned. 'Her dad took her in a taxi.'

'Where?'

'I just told you, home!'

'Without saying goodbye?' I couldn't believe it.

'You know Delia,' Robbie shrugged.

But I realised that I didn't know her at all. When I'd asked Delia why she hadn't even told me she had seven brothers and sisters, she'd said, 'Why does it matter? It's no big deal. I don't have to talk about them all the time.'

'I'm just surprised,' I explained. 'It's so different to my life.'

Delia shrugged.

'I can't imagine sharing my house with so many other kids.'

'Yeah, well, I can't imagine having an inch of space of my own. I only got my own bed for the first time last year. I've always shared with Stacey – since I can remember!' Considering she hadn't talked about it before, once Delia started she couldn't stop. 'Because I'm the oldest, I have to look after them all when Mum's at work – and get their teas – and make sure they do their homework. At least now I get my mum to myself once in a while, that's when she doesn't drag half of them in here with her.'

I realised there must be lots of things Delia had never told me. And to be fair, I hadn't told her things either – like my family secret – even though I'd told Robbie. But I'd still thought we were friends.

'Why didn't she come and *tell* me she was going?' I asked Robbie.

'She probably didn't want to wake you. She was on the phone crying to her mum for nearly an hour. In the end her dad came and collected her. It must have been after eleven.'

Later on in the morning, when Jo came in to

change my bed sheets, I was starting to sound like a recorded message: 'I don't understand. Why didn't she say anything?'

'Don't worry about Delia,' Jo told us. 'There is no way that girl is going to spend the rest of her life in a wheelchair. She has to get out of it and onto crutches. It's going to take a little bit of courage, but that's the only thing that's stopping her.'

'I just feel like I've made things worse,' I told Jo.

'I was the one who hauled her out of her chair,' Robbie reminded me.

'Yes, well...' Jo added, looking at Robbie, 'it's usually better to let people move at their own pace – but you may have done her a favour, giving her a push.'

After Jo left us I was feeling so miserable. I told Robbie, 'Marian's right, I'm just no good at friendship. I shouldn't even bother trying.'

'You haven't exactly had a lot of practice,' Robbie reminded me. 'If you'd spent a fraction of the time you've spent on maths you'd probably be an expert.'

But I knew it wasn't about time. 'It's because there's something wrong with me,' I told him.

'Like *what*?'

I wasn't sure that it was a good idea, but I decided

to tell Robbie anyway – all the things that had been going through my head in the last couple of days.

'You remember me telling you about this Libby? Well, I think she's my mum's sister. I think that's why Grandma got mixed up and called me Libby that time when I was upset. Well, I think Libby might have been mad and that she's locked away somewhere – like Mrs Rochester.'

'What, like in your attic?' Robbie grinned, as if it was a big joke.

'Don't be silly,' I said. 'We don't even have an attic. I mean in an institution, a hospital.'

'Whoa! Where has all this come from? You've been reading too many books, my friend,' Robbie told me. 'You're the one who bangs on about evidence – where's the evidence for any of this?'

'Well, I don't really have any,' I admitted.

'Exactly!'

'But it does add up.'

'How?'

'Because I think my mum may be mad as well.'

'Your mum? Mad?'

'And I think I might be as well,' I admitted, realising

how silly it sounded as soon as I said it out loud. I was quite relieved when Robbie laughed at me.

'You? You're not mad.'

'You're saying that now, but when you first met me I know you and Delia both thought I was odd.'

'Odd's not the same as mad. You're odd for sure, but that's what I like about you. You're not a clone. And your mum doesn't look mad to me, maybe a bit...depressed, but that's different.'

'Is it?' I asked, wanting to believe Robbie, although I couldn't be sure he wasn't just trying to make me feel better. But, actually, I already felt better having told someone else the things that were going round and round in my head.

'You definitely need to get out more,' Robbie told me. 'It doesn't matter what your family's like, you still need to get away from them sometimes.'

'That's easier said than done,' I told him. 'They don't seem to want me to make friends.'

'Perhaps they've got their own reasons.'

'Like what?'

'Don't ask me,' he laughed. 'You're the one with the high IQ; you work it out. Or better still ask them straight out. Get some answers, Einstein. And don't let them pull that woolly hat over your eyes.'

By the time Marian and Grandpa came in to see me, I was in a horrible mood. I wasn't just irritable – I felt *furious*!

Marian noticed straight away. 'I knew that party food would upset you.'

'It's nothing to do with party food,' I told her. 'I'm sick of this bed, and I'm sick of this room, and I'm *bored to death*!'

'I bet you are, flower,' Grandpa said, sympathetically.

But Marian told me, 'You're overtired, that's what it is.'

'Whatever!' I said, exactly like Delia said it.

'What's that supposed to mean?' Marian asked.

It meant that I couldn't be bothered to argue with her, but I couldn't say that without making things worse, so I just looked away.

'I can't believe the change in you,' Marian grumbled. 'I'm not leaving here until I've seen Mr Clarke and got a date for taking you home. The sooner I get you away from this place the better.'

'If you mean away from Delia,' I snapped, 'don't waste your time; she's gone already.'

'Well, maybe that's a good thing.'

I couldn't believe Marian had said that. I'd lost my first real friend and she didn't seem to care. But when she saw how upset I was she said, 'Oh, sweetheart. I knew you'd get hurt.'

'I'm not hurt,' I insisted. I didn't want to admit that Marian was right, even though *hurt* was exactly what I felt. It was like the time when Grandpa turned against me – I thought it must be my fault. Surely Delia wouldn't have just disappeared like that, without saying goodbye, unless I'd upset her?

I was glad when Grandpa changed the subject and asked Marian to go and get him a cup of coffee.

'Can't you go yourself, Dad?' she asked, irritably. But he only got irritable back until, to keep the peace, Marian went off to the café and left us together.

The minute she was out of the room, Grandpa shot over to sit by my bed. He clutched my hand and said, 'I've got something to tell you. It's a secret. You can keep a secret, can't you?'

'You know I can,' I said, quietly. At last I was going to get the information I was so desperate for.

Grandpa took a deep breath and I suddenly felt scared. I had this terrible feeling that if it was something really bad I might not want to know, after all. I took a deep breath too, but I could have saved myself the worry.

'I've had to hide some of my orchid bulbs.'

'Your orchid bulbs? Why, Grandpa?' I asked.

He took another deep breath and looked into my eyes. I think he was still trying to decide if he could trust me.

'I won't say anything,' I promised.

'Those bulbs, the ones I lost after the accident... someone handed them in. Now the *orchid police* have got hold of them. We're going to get visited!'

'When?'

'Any day soon, probably.'

'So where have you hidden them?' I asked.

'Where the devils won't find them,' he whispered, as if the room was bugged. 'In The Log – under the throne.'

I couldn't believe he'd go there without asking me. 'You didn't move anything, did you?' I didn't want him finding my box of Grandma's things and looking inside. But he shook his head. 'I'm sorry, I didn't think you'd mind; I couldn't think of anywhere else. Luckily someone tipped me off in time.'

Grandpa sounded like he was caught up in some

spy story. I didn't know how much of his story to believe. I thought it might all be in his imagination; probably my accident had pushed him, as well as Marian, over the edge. I suddenly felt like I was surrounded by mad people.

'You won't tell your mum, will you? It's our secret?'

'No, I won't, Grandpa,' I promised, 'if you tell me what the other secret is, the one that Marian was arguing with you about keeping from me, that has something to do with me.'

Grandpa's face clouded over and he pulled away from me. He wouldn't even look me in the eye. In fact, he got up out of the chair, looking really agitated.

'If your mother's not telling you something she must have her reasons, Chloe. Right now she's got enough on her plate. I wouldn't advise you to go upsetting her, OK?'

Before I could ask anything else, Marian came back with Grandpa's cup of coffee and he moved his chair back in the corner, but he kept nodding at me as if we had this pact now. Marian could tell something had happened and she tried to catch my eye, but I looked away.

Right then I really wanted Daniel to be there, someone a bit more normal, but Marian had already told me that he'd been working on his presentation until the early hours and he really had to keep going. He'd come in as soon as he'd finished.

I felt so angry with all of them: with Daniel, for not coming to see me, with Grandpa for going into my private space to hide his stupid orchids, but with Marian most of all. I knew Grandpa was right about not pushing her, but I wasn't going to let her leave without me getting at least one question off my chest. When she got up and started sorting through my things, putting my clean clothes away, I thought, it's now or never.

In fact it was easier than I'd expected – a bit like stepping off the bus actually, without worrying what might be coming. I just said it, all in a rush, 'What would be so bad about me going to school, Marian? Why are you *so* determined you don't want me to? What are you afraid of?'

Marian sort of gasped in a load of air, as if I'd punched her. 'Where on earth did that come from? Honestly, Chloe, as if we haven't got enough on our minds without bringing something like that up now.'

Grandpa suddenly joined in. 'Well, maybe it's important to Chloe. Have you considered that? Perhaps this is one thing you *could* talk to her about.'

'Don't start, Dad,' Marian warned Grandpa, through clenched teeth. She was really wound up, but she carried on folding my clothes, trying to keep calm. 'We'll talk about it another time, when we're on our own,' she said looking over her shoulder at Grandpa. 'And when *you're* in a better place, Chloe, and have had enough sleep. It's not as if I didn't warn you that party wasn't a good idea.'

But I wasn't going to wait. 'Why can't you tell me now? I'm asking you a simple question: why don't you want me to go?'

Marian stopped folding clothes and turned to me with her eyes full up. 'You know that I've only ever wanted to keep you safe. That's all I've ever cared about.'

'What's that got to do with anything?' I said. 'We're talking about me going to *school*, not on safari!'

But I didn't get any further. Marian refused to say any more on the subject. As they were leaving, Grandpa came and gave my hand a squeeze and winked at me. I could see by her face that Marian thought the two of us were ganging up on her, as usual, but by that point I didn't really care.

Robbie didn't come back in to see me until much later, after his mum and dad had left and it was nearly lights out. He was in a funny mood too. He didn't really listen when I told him how things had gone with Marian.

'What's wrong with you?' I asked. 'Are you worried about tomorrow?'

'I tried to persuade my parents to let me go home. Put it off till after the trials.'

'What happened?'

'The usual: they got upset and begged me to get it done, then I got upset and gave in.'

We sat quietly together for a while, until Trish put her head round the door, looking for Robbie.

'You've got an early start tomorrow,' she reminded him. 'You should really get to bed.' She hovered around, waiting for Robbie.

'By the time I see you again, I might be off traction,' I said. 'I hope it goes OK tomorrow.'

'Have you still got any of those chocolates left, the ones Gemma gave you?' Robbie suddenly asked.

'They're in my locker.'

'You're on starvation from midnight,' Trish reminded him.

'Yeah, yeah, nil by mouth,' Robbie said. 'But surely I can have something to look forward to afterwards.'

'Hope they cheer you up,' I said, passing him the box.

'Oh, they will,' he told me, grinning. 'You're a real mate.'

Trish disappeared and Robbie just stopped long enough to remind me what we'd agreed: to stand firm – both of us.

'I will,' I promised, 'if you will.'

'Oh, I'm going to, from this moment on,' he said, with a real look in his eye. 'And you make sure you get those answers.'

To be honest, the longer it went on, the more scared I was starting to feel about what those answers might be. But I'd made a deal with Robbie, and I couldn't go back on it now. I promised myself that nothing would stop me getting to the bottom of Marian's secret and this time I really meant it.

Chapter Eighteen

Contradictory Ideas

There is a method that mathematicians sometimes use, called PROOF BY CONTRADICTION, which involves trying to prove that a theorem is true by first assuming that it's false.

Euclid, when he was trying to establish the idea of irrational numbers, set out to prove that the square root of 2 could not be written as a fraction.

He did this by first trying to prove that it could.

When there was a contradiction in his proof and he came up with an absurd result, this proved, he said, that his original idea was correct and that the square root of 2 must be an irrational number.

Daniel says that in Latin this method is called *reductio ad absurdum*, which literally means 'reduction to the impossible', which sounds pretty silly when you think about it. But when he told me about it, I found myself trying something a bit similar.

In the time after Grandma died, but before my accident, when I'd been spending a lot more time on my own on The Log, trying to *de-tragify* and rewrite my own family story, sometimes I would start further back when I was about six. Instead of giving up on school, I imagined myself carrying on going and not being home-schooled.

In this version I didn't feel different from the other kids, or nervous of them, because I had lots of friends, or at least quite a few. I wasn't particularly clever, just average, and I never got called *weirdo*, because I wasn't. I fitted in and did ordinary things like playing with dolls and trying on make-up and listening to pop music, like Hayley, and watching lots of TV – like Delia. I wasn't into maths, I thought it was a bit boring – like they do. I wasn't really into anything in a big way.

I imagined myself in a different kind of family too. Marian didn't breed orchids and Daniel didn't do mathematical research. In fact, this imaginary family didn't have anything special about it; it was just quite ordinary.

Afterwards, though, I was always surprised by how dissatisfied I felt with these made-up versions. It was a bit like with the books I'd tried to *de-tragify* in the past: once I'd taken out the sad and scary bits, they fell apart or turned out pretty dull. That's how this imagined life seemed – *too* ordinary. But the main problem was that I couldn't recognise myself in it, it didn't seem to be *my* life any more.

Even if I hadn't been completely happy since Grandma died, I couldn't believe that I'd have been any happier in this other, different, made-up life. I think I would probably have been...bored.

I wasn't sure whether *proof by contradiction* only works in maths, or if it's supposed to work in life too. But I'd rewritten my life so that it was the complete opposite of what it actually was, and it felt completely wrong. Was that telling me that my life had actually been right in the first place?

Again, after I ended up in hospital, I tried to imagine my life if the accident hadn't happened, but that felt contradictory too. I didn't want to have had an accident and upset everyone and have my life turned upside down, of course I didn't, but without the accident I would never have met Robbie and Delia. I would have been too scared of upsetting Marian to bring up the subject of going to school. I'd have just kept on as I was, hoping everything would get back to normal and waiting for that to happen. I would never have overheard Marian and Grandpa talking about the family secret. I might have stayed in the dark about that...forever. Did that make it *a happy accident*, then?

On the other hand, without it, my head wouldn't have been full of all these difficult questions and I wouldn't have had to face whatever it was they'd been trying to keep from me. Perhaps I'd have been happier that way.

But once I knew that there was a secret – that had something to do with me – I couldn't pretend that I didn't. Like Robbie said, all I could do now was just get on with it – and get those answers.

Chapter Nineteen

I was in a horrible mood when I woke the next morning. If I'd been at home, I would have stayed in my pyjamas and wrapped myself in a blanket and found somewhere to curl up all day and read. But since I was in hospital, and had no choice about whether to stay in my pyjamas or where to curl up, I felt like having a good scream instead. Obviously I didn't.

There seemed to be a lot going on outside my door, but no one came in to see me. I wasn't expecting to see Robbie; he'd probably gone down for his op already. All I had to look forward to was a long boring day on my own. When Jo finally came in she looked as cross as I was feeling.

'Has Robbie gone down to theatre?' I asked.

'Obviously not!' she said sharply.

I didn't know what that meant.

'You needn't look so innocent,' she said, tugging my bedclothes about.

I looked at her blankly.

'I must say, Chloe, if you're pretending, you're doing it very well,' she said, giving me one of her laser-looks.

'I'm not pretending,' I told her, indignantly. 'I don't do that.'

Jo didn't seem to know whether to believe me. 'Well, that friend of yours is in big trouble – with *me*, the doctors *and* his parents, who are coming in right this minute. So if you did have any part in it, I'd advise you to keep your head down.'

'Like I have any choice,' I muttered, but Jo had already turned her back.

Half an hour later, when I was beginning to feel as if every minute of the day was going to drag endlessly on, a head popped round the door, grinning.

'What's going on?' I demanded. 'What's happened to your op?'

'Been cancelled,' Robbie told me, coming in and closing the door. He looked so pleased with himself he was almost bouncing.

'How? Why? What happened?'

'Queen of the Questions still,' Robbie grinned. 'I sabotaged it. I ate your chocolates – the whole box. Sorry,' he said, 'but it was in a good cause.'

I couldn't believe he'd done it. But Robbie explained that he'd stayed awake all night thinking of nothing else. He knew if he told anyone they'd just try to persuade him, whereas if he ate the chocolates they'd have to cancel.

'Jo gave me this big lecture about wasting NHS time and money,' he told me. 'My folks both cried, but I know they'll get over it. The consultant said if I'd explained to him in the first place about the trials, he'd have understood. Anyway, they're going to reschedule it in a few weeks' time. I'm off now, but I didn't want to do a Delia, and leave without saying goodbye.'

'You're not going home too?' I said. I hardly ever cry but suddenly I was sniffing back tears.

'Hey, whoa, whoa. Don't worry, you haven't seen the last of me. I'll write to you; I might even brave your mum and come and visit. And listen, thanks, I'd never have done this without your help. Now it's your turn. Get those answers.'

I was already feeling scared but now, if the secret

turned out to be something really bad, I wouldn't even have Robbie to talk to about it. How would I manage to decide what to do about school without him, I asked?

'I thought you'd made that decision,' he said. 'Just do it. Go on.'

'I can't,' I said. 'I keep changing my mind.'

'Then I'll make it for you. You're going to school. Right? You have to, unless you want to spend the rest of your life under your mum's thumb.'

That didn't feel quite right, but there was no time left to argue with Robbie, because Jo came in to say his parents were ready to leave.

'Remember,' he said, 'stay strong and get some answers, Einstein.'

I tried to smile back but I couldn't. Robbie took off his baseball cap and handed it to me. 'For your hat collection,' he said and suddenly he was gone too.

I decided that saying goodbye to Robbie wasn't any easier than having Delia disappear on me. Both gave me a pain in my stomach.

I lay in bed, thinking about what Robbie had just said about me being under Marian's thumb. It must have looked like that to him, that she was always keeping me from doing things, but that was only one side of Marian. Robbie didn't know the other side like I did.

I remembered some of our best voyages of discovery – to castles and theatres and bird reserves. There was one time we made pirate hats and acted out storming the stockade on Treasure Island, and turned The Log into a galleon and made up a play about Christopher Columbus discovering America. Once we turned the dining room into a natural history museum with dinosaur models, and bird and animal skeletons. Grandma called it *Chloe's Little Shop of Horrors*. Marian let me leave it like that for a whole month so we had to eat off our knees in the sitting room.

Marian had always been my best friend and my best teacher, as well as my mum. I suddenly realised that if I went to school we wouldn't have those days again. I was starting to feel really homesick.

When Gemma came in and suggested we do some art together, I agreed to do a collage, even though tearing and sticking seems to me like the most pointless thing in the world. She talked a lot about her wedding, which was coming up soon, so to change the subject I asked her opinion about school.

'Oh, school's OK,' she said. 'You'd do well at school, being so clever. I never was. But there were plenty of things I liked: cooking and sewing…and art. And, of course, I had lots of friends.'

Well, I do lots of cooking and bits of sewing already at home. And I can certainly live without art, especially *collage*, but friends – that was the thing.

The day dragged on and on and I regretted telling Marian and Daniel they needn't come in so much. When Jo popped in to tell me there'd been a message to say they were going to be late, I could hardly stop the tears.

Jo was really surprised. 'Oh, Chloe, what is it? This isn't like you. I'm sorry, I shouldn't have said that stuff this morning about Robbie. It's OK. He told me you had nothing to do with it.'

I shook my head. I didn't know where to start explaining what I was feeling. Even though I was crying, more than anything else I felt angry again. I seemed to be feeling angry a lot at the moment.

I was angry that Delia and Robbie had been able to go home and I was still there, left on my own. Angry with the consultant who, every time I asked when I could come off traction said: 'soon', but it still hadn't happened. Angry with Jo for thinking I'd been lying about Robbie, and angry with Gemma for not being able to come up with anything more interesting to do than another stupid collage!

But it was my family I was most angry with over this stupid secret. What right did they have to keep it from me if it had big implications for me, and my life? What was the point of me trying to decide whether to go to school if I was never going to be able to fit in anyway? Marian and Daniel always talked about respect – about trusting me to make my own choices and decisions – about us being a team. And all the time they'd been keeping secrets from me.

Finally I was so exhausted with frustration I must have dozed off, because suddenly they were in the room, standing over my bed, and for a moment it felt like another of my dreams. But then I realised I was awake.

Marian was looking even worse; her eyes were red-rimmed, as if she'd been crying, and her face looked puffy. Both of them looked as if they hadn't slept very well. Daniel hadn't shaved and his hair needed cutting. I could see why the nurses were always giving them sideways looks.

But then Marian leaned over me and gave me a hug and I found myself clinging onto her and, only by hiding my head in her coat, managed not to burst into tears. Daniel came over and hugged me too and said, 'Hello, sweetie, we're so sorry to be late.'

But before I had chance to tell them that Robbie had gone home and that now I was all on my own, they were already explaining why they were late.

'There's been a little bit of bother with your grandpa,' Daniel started.

But Marian cut in, 'Bit of bother?! That's an understatement, Daniel. It's a disaster, that's what it is. We could lose the whole nursery because of his stupidity.'

'I'm sure that isn't going to happen,' Daniel reassured her.

I sighed and wondered what Grandpa had done *now*. Marian was actually crying, so Daniel had to explain.

Apparently, that morning, while Marian was still having breakfast, two officials from CITES – Grandpa's *orchid police* – had turned up and insisted on searching the whole nursery. They wouldn't actually say what they were looking for, but they'd told Marian they'd been *alerted* when a brown paper parcel of orchid bulbs from Guatemala was handed into the local police station.

Daniel said it had all been quite reasonable at first, but when they'd started turning Grandpa's hothouses upside down and he had threatened to thump one of them, things had turned more serious.

'Thankfully, they didn't actually arrest him,' Daniel said, smiling.

'But they threatened they'd be back,' Marian said. 'I've always known something like this was going to happen. I'm always telling you, Chloe, aren't I?'

I hadn't said a word throughout the story, because my mind was piecing together all the bits Grandpa had told me. I thought he'd been talking rubbish, but he'd been right, after all. He'd hidden those bulbs just in time by the sound of things. I should have stayed quiet, but I couldn't help asking, 'Did they look anywhere else? Apart from the greenhouses?'

No, Daniel shook his head. He didn't think that was an odd question, but I could see that Marian did.

'You don't look entirely surprised, Chloe,' she said. 'Did you know about any of this? Has your grandfather been confiding in you?'

I didn't know what to say. I thought about Jo

accusing me of *pretending* earlier on and me denying that I ever did it. But here I was now ready to lie to my mum. I didn't want to take sides, but I wasn't sure what Marian would do if I told her where Grandpa's bulbs were hidden. I didn't want to add to his troubles and I didn't want to break his confidence, even though at the time I hadn't realised that he seriously was confiding in me.

I didn't trust myself to lie very well, so I shook my head, and tried to look innocent, but Marian wasn't fooled.

'I don't think you realise what a serious business this is, Chloe,' she said.

'I'm sure Chloe does,' Daniel said, peacekeeping again.

'I wouldn't like to think you've been keeping secrets from us,' Marian went on.

Well, that was just the worst thing she could have said to me. The little sparks of anger I'd been feeling all day seemed to be growing into a full-sized fire inside me. I think Daniel could sense what was coming, because he suddenly tried to change the subject and calm us both down.

'Look, Marian, let's leave all that for now. Chloe wanted to talk about school, that's what we're here for.' He was looking from one of us to the other, but Marian and I were staring at each other and the tension between us was almost crackling like electricity.

'What we need to do is to approach the subject with an open mind...' Daniel bumbled on, like I do sometimes, even when no one's listening. I realised that was probably where I got it from.

I was beginning to feel dizzy, and a bit sick. In fact, when I finally opened my mouth it was quite like being sick; I couldn't have stopped myself if I'd tried. I had no idea what the words were going to be. They all came out in a rush and cut Daniel off mid-sentence.

'Forget about school!' I shouted. 'Who cares about that? What I want to know is: who's Libby and what's happened to her?

'Where is she?

'Why does no one ever talk about her?

'Was *she* mad like Marian?'

And finally I almost screamed at them, 'But most of all what I want to know is, why has no one ever told *me*? Is it because I'm mad as well?'

I don't think Marian or Daniel quite knew what had hit them. They both looked as if they'd been run down by a four-by-four and I'd been the one driving it. Marian's breathing was loud and snatched and I thought any minute we were going to need to call one of the nurses to her; Daniel looked like someone had knocked him sideways.

But me? I felt much better, even though I hadn't got any answers – *yet*.

Chapter Twenty
The Complete Story

One of the basic principles in mathematics is that, in theory at least, every question must have an answer. Mathematicians call this concept COMPLETENESS.

In the beginning, when only whole numbers existed and mathematicians were faced with the problem of 2 divided by 8, the need for completeness eventually led to the discovery of fractions. Later, to answer the question: what is the square root of 2, the need for completeness led mathematicians to discover irrational numbers. In the same way, to answer the question: 2 minus 8, negative numbers had to be devised, in order to satisfy this need for completeness.

And that seems really neat to me!

Daniel had often talked to me about the idea of *completeness*, but I'd begun to think it was another idea that may only be true for maths. In life, I'd decided, Robbie was probably right – lots of problems simply don't have a solution. After all, Robbie had been right about other things.

He was definitely right when he told me that I should have asked the questions sooner. Instead I'd made up that whole crazy imaginary story about us all being mad – for *completeness* I suppose. It obviously hadn't worked, though, because still nothing felt complete – or sorted – in any way.

Maybe now that I have got the real story, though, there's a chance that things will finally feel sorted.

Robbie had been right about the madness too, wouldn't you know? To be honest the only bit of the story I did get right was that Libby *was* someone's sister. No, not Marian's. *Mine!*

I still can't quite believe it: I had a sister that I've never known about! She would have been twenty-one now – if she'd lived. I keep trying to imagine myself with a big sister called Libby.

If I was at home now, telling you this story, I'd have probably dressed in black, but I would have worn my pink hat, to cheer me up. We'd probably have gone out onto The Log and taken Sir Walter Raleigh with us for a bit of comfort. And we'd definitely have needed a big box of tissues between us, because it's an absolutely tragic story. There's no point trying to *de-tragify* it because this all really happened. Marian and Daniel told me the whole story between them.

Marian met Daniel when they were students at university. I've seen photos of them; they were both a bit hippyish with long curly hair, exactly the same colour as mine; they looked a bit like brother and sister – much more alike than Marian and her own brother, Steve. They were both really clever, regular Einsteins as Robbie would say, but halfway through her course Marian found she was pregnant and had to drop out of her course.

Marian was just like me, Daniel said, she loved studying, and she found it really hard to give up. She wanted to have the baby, but she wanted to study as well. It made her quite angry and I can understand that, because Daniel didn't have to give up his course, did he?

But then, after Libby was born, it began to look as if he might have to as well. Daniel didn't get much of a grant, so he took a job working in a petrol station at nights and sometimes at weekends. He got so tired, trying to study at the same time, that he nearly dropped out too.

That's where my uncle Steve comes in. I find it quite strange calling him that, because I've never even met him, but I suppose that doesn't change the fact that he's still my uncle. Uncle Steve is five years older than Marian and they'd never really got on. He was always teasing her and playing tricks on her and making her feel stupid. He was a typical older brother, Marian says.

By this time Uncle Steve was married with a wife, called Suzy, and two children, Mark and Cassie, my cousins, although I've never met them, either. He had a successful computer company and they had a big house near Oxford – with a swimming pool! So he suggested that Marian and Daniel move in with them and Marian would look after all the children so that Suzy could go to college too.

Marian said it was horrible for her. She didn't get on with Steve, and she hated the fact that everyone else was doing what they wanted to – except her.

It's hard for me to imagine now, because Marian was always so good at teaching me and coming up with exciting things to do, but then she was only nineteen and she didn't enjoy staying at home, looking after children. She found lots of ways to keep them quiet: sitting them in front of TV, or watching videos, anything which gave her a little time to herself – to sneak off with her books. But Marian says that's only a small thing to forgive herself, compared to what happened next.

It was a hot, sticky day in June. Mark and Cassie by this time were eight and six, and they had just come home from school. Marian was studying, while Libby, who was nearly four, was still having an afternoon nap. Mark and Cassie wanted to go in the swimming pool but Marian told them they had to wait until Libby finished her nap, and she'd finished her reading.

'Oh, please,' Mark begged, 'just to cool off.'

But Marian said, 'No, you must wait till Libby wakes up.'

Mostly, Marian says, Mark and Cassie did as they were told, but it was hot and they were tired and irritable.

Marian heard Libby start to cry, but Mark called to her, 'It's OK, Libby's awake, we'll get her up.' And then things went quiet.

Marian kept on reading, she's not sure for how long, but suddenly she heard another sound, a different kind of cry – Mark's voice, she thinks, but something about it made her go straight out.

Mark and Cassie were coming towards her, wearing their wet swimsuits, their eyes big and round with terror. They looked frozen and they were holding onto one another.

Marian thought, 'What an old ogre they must think I am to be so afraid I'll kick up a fuss,' and she broke out into a smile.

'It's OK,' she told them, 'I'm not going to have a fit *this time*. But you should have waited, like I told you to.'

She turned to get them a towel each, because she could see they were shivering. It was only as she went back into the house that it occurred to her to wonder where Libby was.

A little child like Libby can drown in a paddling pool, or even in a puddle, Daniel told me – in a matter of minutes. It's far easier in a swimming pool, especially if she trips over a piece of hose and bangs her head on the side and is already concussed when she falls in the water.

I don't suppose a little child like that would make much noise, not much more than a splash, so when two children are practising diving at the other end of the pool and arguing, it is possible they wouldn't notice until it was too late. Nobody blamed them, anyway; they were only children.

Daniel had to finish the story because by then Marian was crying as if she'd never stop. I wanted to go over and give her a hug, but I was still stuck in my bed on traction. Marian looked over at me, as if she couldn't move from her chair either, but through her tears she gave me a little smile. And I gave her the biggest smile back I could manage.

I suddenly felt like Jo: as if I could see inside Marian's head and understand for the first time what she was thinking and why she sometimes behaved the way she did.

By now we were all crying. Daniel was crying without making a sound and I was crying, but I couldn't help smiling at the same time, thinking about the sister I never knew I had. I wondered what she would have looked like, what sort of a person she was, what kind of friends we would have been, what different kind of life I might have had if Libby hadn't drowned.

Later on, Trish came in and was so kind to Marian. She took her into the parents' room for a while, and made her a cup of tea until she stopped crying.

'When something terrible happens like that nothing can make it OK, or even easier,' Daniel told me, 'but if there's a reason, an explanation, even someone else to blame, it can sometimes make it more bearable.'

But this wasn't like that. It was an accident. A terrible tragic accident and there was no one to blame – except Marian. She knew she should have been there and she would never forgive herself – ever, I could see that.

Suddenly it was easy to see why she'd always been so overprotective of me. Why she'd tried to keep me close to her. Why she'd hated me going to school.

'Now I understand why Marian didn't want me to go swimming those times with Grandma,' I told Daniel. 'That must have been really hard for her. But why,' I asked him, 'did you have to keep it a secret? Did you really think I couldn't have handled it?'

Daniel shook his head. 'None of it was ever about protecting you, Chloe. We were always trying to protect Marian.'

I nodded. Daniel took hold of my hand.

'And, in case you're still worrying,' he added, 'sometimes Marian feels very, very sad, but that doesn't make her mad, nor was Libby, and neither are you, my darling – even if sometimes you do jump to crazy conclusions.'

Chapter Twenty-One

It's amazing how different a room seems when you look at it from a completely different angle. For over a month I'd been used to seeing it lying down so on my first day sitting in a chair, it felt like discovering a whole new place. I hadn't known what the weather had been for weeks, but it suddenly seemed spring-like. If I'd been at home it was just the kind of day I'd have broken out into shorts and T-shirt and run around squealing.

They'd taken the traction down the day before and Mr Clarke told me, 'It'll be quite a while before you're running anywhere, Chloe. You'll need a lot more physio first, but I think we can let you go home in a day or two.'

I couldn't wait to get home. I'd missed it so much. I'd almost forgotten what The Log looked like, and what Sir Walter Raleigh's fur felt like against my face, and the smell of Grandpa's *Stanhopeas* mixed with his cigars.

I'd forgotten so many other things too. All my maths seemed to have disappeared out of that hole in my brain. I was looking forward to getting back to teatimes with Daniel. Marian had brought in some muffins that she'd made, but they weren't as good as mine – even my slightly over-baked ones – still warm from the oven.

Half way through the morning, when the post arrived on the ward, Jo brought me in a letter from Robbie. I'd already had a card from Delia; it was sitting on my bedside locker. In it she'd told me she was coming to see me one day that week, when she started back at the hospital school. They'd told her she could finish the school year there, if she kept on with the crutches.

'I'm getting used to them,' she told me, 'but I still hate them. They don't half make my arms ache. Anyway my mum says I shouldn't overdo it.' She'd signed it: your best friend Dee.

I opened Robbie's letter and read bits out to Jo. It was full of chat about football, because he said he knew how interested I was in it – ha, ha!

He said he'd got through the first trials, the next were coming up later that week so we'd all got to keep everything crossed for him. And he finished off by saying, 'Hope you've got all the answers at last!'

Jo gave me one of those head-on-one-side looks. 'And have you?'

I didn't want to go into all that again, so I just shrugged and nodded, which was suddenly so much easier now I was sitting up.

I wasn't sure whether I'd got *all* the answers, but I knew as much as I needed to know, for now at least.

I'd told Marian that I really did understand how hard it must have been for her and how sorry I was. And she'd had another big cry – and then so had I.

I suppose I'd always realised, without knowing why, that Marian needed looking after and that I should try to avoid upsetting her. I wasn't sure that it would make so much difference now that I knew the reason why, but I was glad that I did know. I think secrets are usually a bad idea.

'I bet you're looking forward to going home,' Jo said.

'Oh, yes,' I sighed, 'I can't wait.'

'Nice to get back to normal, eh?'

I smiled, but I wasn't completely sure what that

meant, because I still hadn't decided the other big question: school or not?

'For every reason I can think of to go to school,' I told Jo, 'I think of another one for staying at home. It's like a set of scales perfectly balanced.' I sighed. 'Maybe Daniel has some equation that would give me the answer.'

Jo smiled. 'Well, I know nothing about equations, but I think you're trying to answer a question which might not need an answer and missing a much more important one.'

I looked back at her, like she often looked at me, with my head on one side. Jo came and sat down beside me.

'It doesn't seem to me this question is really to do with your education. It isn't a question of school or not: it's a question of friends or not. You don't have to go to school to find those. Now you know you can do it there are lots of places you can find friends. You just need to go out and look for them a little more.'

I suddenly found that a really scary idea. I'd never been very brave about it, but after a month in a hospital bed, even sitting up in a chair felt like an adventure.

'Just give yourself a little time,' Jo said. 'You've done the important bit already.'

Jo took Robbie's card off me and put it beside Delia's. Then she took my wrist and checked my pulse. 'Considering how scary it sometimes seems, the world's a very safe place,' she told me. She kept on looking into my eyes. 'You may not believe in God, Chloe, but from now on I think you're going to believe in yourself much more.'

When Marian and Daniel came in later they were so pleased to find me sitting in a chair, they both rushed over and hugged me at the same time. Marian's eyes were full of tears again, but she looked different. She was still a bit pale and anxious, but now she looked more like someone getting over the flu, than someone going down with it.

Daniel definitely looked happier, like maybe he'd had a breakthrough with his research, but when I asked him that he said, 'Too early to tell.'

I hadn't noticed Grandpa at first, because he was hanging back a bit, but when I did I was so pleased to see him I almost jumped out of my chair. He came over and hugged me so hard he nearly lifted me out of it.

'They didn't find them, then?' I whispered in his ear.

He shook his head and whispered back, 'No way. Those idiots couldn't find their way out of a paper bag.'

I was secretly glad Grandpa had outwitted the *orchid police*.

'What are you two whispering about?' Marian asked.

'Nothing,' I fibbed. 'I'm glad they didn't put you in jail – on bread and water,' I told Grandpa.

'Even if they had, I'd have broken out,' Grandpa said, 'rather than miss this celebration.'

'Don't even joke about it, Dad,' Marian frowned at him. 'They might be back yet.'

Grandpa had been carrying a carrier bag and now he put it on the floor and took out a box – one of his Cuban cigar-boxes – and held it against his chest. He took a deep breath and cleared his throat, like he might be about to give a little speech.

'I'm very relieved to hear that things are out in the open at last. I have to say, if everyone had listened to me in the first place...'

'Yes, yes, OK, Dad,' Marian interrupted him. 'Let's not go into all that.'

Grandpa nodded and offered the box to me. I looked from Marian to Daniel trying to tell from their expressions what this was about. All I could think was that he'd brought his illegal orchid bulbs in for me to hide here in hospital. But, surely, Marian wouldn't be smiling if that were the case.

As soon as I held the box I knew that it wasn't orchid bulbs, it felt far too light. Then I had the horrible idea that this might be Grandma's box. I knew Grandpa must have seen it when he hid his bulbs in The Log, but surely he wouldn't have moved that? It was private. I didn't want anyone else to see what I'd put in there. But as well as that, everyone was smiling and cheerful for a change, and I didn't want us all to be plunged into gloom again.

My stomach suddenly went into a sort of squeeze. I thought, oh no, is this some other secret they've been keeping from me? I didn't want any more surprises to deal with. I sat studying the box lid as if it might give me some clue what was inside, but it didn't and I didn't have X-ray eyes.

I looked at Grandpa, but he just nodded in an encouraging sort of way, so in the end I had to trust him.

I rested the box on my knee and lifted the lid. Inside was a little pile of things. On top sat a very small teddy, a bit chewed-looking, with a rather ragged ribbon round its neck. I lifted it up and couldn't help smiling. Without thinking I rested it against my cheek and it just fitted there, under my ear, and felt sort of comforting somehow.

Under the teddy was a little pair of white baby's bootees tied together by their ribbons. Then a couple of photographs of me as a little girl: one as a toddler where I'm holding Daniel's hand and just starting to walk – he's still got all that hippyish long fair hair – and another one where I'm maybe four and sitting on Grandpa's shoulders. I'd never seen either of them before, but I could recognise myself from other old photos – or I thought I could.

And then I lifted out a little plastic bracelet, the sort babies wear when they're first born in hospital. I'd often seen mine, Marian kept it in her bedside drawer. But as soon as I picked it up, before I even turned it over and read the name, my intuition told me that it wasn't mine, that this one was going to say: Libby Wells, born 7th June, 1985, wt 3.23 kg.

'Your grandma kept this box,' Grandpa told me. 'She always hoped that one day she'd be able to share it with you, if the day ever came when it wasn't too painful for your mum.'

I tried to look at everyone still standing round me,

smiling, but I couldn't see them properly because my eyes were suddenly full of tears.

All I could think was: I'm not an only one. Even though I'd never met Libby, even though she'd died, I was in a set of sisters.

Afterwards, Grandpa reached again into his carrier bag and took out an orchid. I thought, oh dear, Jo won't be pleased. But I quickly realised that this wasn't just any other orchid. I'd seen this one before. I recognised it from the high shelf in Grandpa's hothouses. It was so pretty you couldn't easily forget it. It had lots of star-like flowers, creamy-green coloured, like the flesh of an apple. This time Grandpa let me read the label. Its name was *Little Libby*.

At least I'd been right about that.

But Grandpa wasn't finished yet, he was smiling like a magician who still has another trick in his bag. It was *another* orchid.

'Came into flower this morning,' he said, 'for the first time,' and his voice was trembling with excitement. 'I have waited seven years for this little beauty and I think you'll agree it was worth the wait.'

He said that it was from the same parent plant as Libby's. The flowers on this one were a little bit smaller, but a richer colour, tinted with pink. It was even more perfect, if that's possible, and it smelled... heavenly. Grandma would have approved.

Grandpa handed me an empty label and a marker pen.

'Let's have a Naming Ceremony. Your very best handwriting now, Chloe.'

I shook my head. 'You do it, Grandpa. You know my writing isn't a patch on yours.'

'Rubbish,' he said, holding them out again. 'Come on, like I've shown you.'

'What's it going to be called?' I asked him, taking the pen.

'What do you think to *Libby's Little Sister*?'

I thought it was perfect and I wrote it as carefully as I could, in my very best copperplate handwriting.

I looked up and smiled at Marian and I just knew that things would be different from now on. How could they not be?

Sometimes when you've worked on a maths problem, or a puzzle, for ages and suddenly all the pieces fall into place, it seems so obvious and you can't imagine how you didn't see it in the first place. You really kick yourself for missing the clues. But that's looking at it backwards, with the answer in front of you.

Life can be like that too.

But that's all right. What I've learnt is: it doesn't really matter how long it takes, or how you get there – as long as you get the answer in the end.

More Orchard Red Apples

Utterly Me, Clarice Bean	Lauren Child	1 84362 304 8
Clarice Bean Spells Trouble	Lauren Child	1 84362 858 9
The Truth Cookie	Fiona Dunbar	1 84362 549 0
Cupid Cakes	Fiona Dunbar	1 84362 688 8
Chocolate Wishes	Fiona Dunbar	1 84362 689 6
The Truth About Josie Green	Belinda Hollyer	1 84362 885 6
My Scary Fairy Godmother	Rose Impey	1 84362 683 7
Shooting Star	Rose Impey	1 84362 560 1
You're Amazing Mr Jupiter	Sue Limb	1 84362 614 4
Do Not Read This Book	Pat Moon	1 84121 435 3
Do Not Read Any Further	Pat Moon	1 84121 456 6
Do Not Read Or Else	Pat Moon	1 84616 082 0
Tower Block Pony	Alison Prince	1 84362 648 9
What Howls at the Moon in Frilly Knickers?	Emily Smith	1 84121 808 1
When Mum Threw Out the Telly	Emily Smith	1 84121 810 3

All priced at £4.99

Orchard Red Apples are available from all good bookshops, or can be ordered direct
from the publisher: Orchard Books, PO BOX 29, Douglas IM99 1BQ
Credit card orders please telephone 01624 836000
or fax 01624 837033 or visit our Internet site: www.wattspub.co.uk
or e-mail: bookshop@enterprise.net for details.

To order please quote title, author and ISBN
and your full name and address.
Cheques and postal orders should be made payable to 'Bookpost plc.'
Postage and packing is FREE within the UK
(overseas customers should add £1.00 per book).

Prices and availability are subject to change.